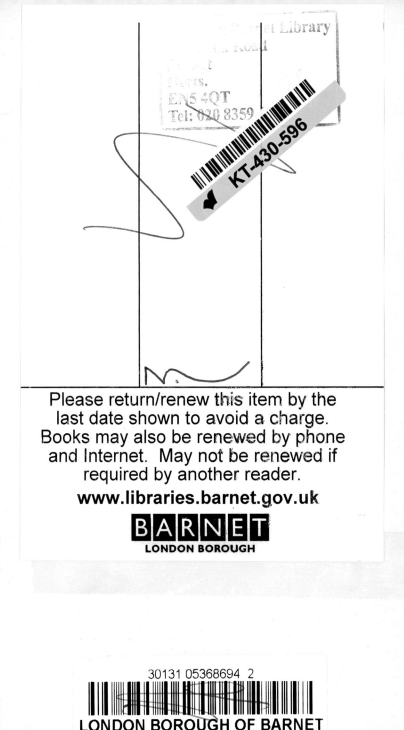

MORRISSEY

List of the Lost

PENGUIN BOOKS

The author would like to thank Helen Conford

PENGUIN BOOKS

UK | USA | Canada | Ireland | Australia

India | New Zealand | South Africa

Penguin Books is part of the Penguin Random House group of companies whose addresses can be found at global.penguinrandomhouse.com.

First published 2015

001

Author photograph copyright © Michael Muller/CPi Syndication

Cover photograph copyright © AP/PA Images: Earl Young of Abilene Christian is about to break the tape to win the 440 yard relay at the Penn Relays in Philadelphia, upsetting favourites Villanova, who finished second with Frank Budd; April 28, 1962.

Set in Garamond Mt Std 12.5pt/14.75pt by Penguin Books
Printed in Great Britain by Clays Ltd, St Ives plc

A CIP catalogue record for this book is available from the British Library

ISBN: 978–0–141–98296–0

www.greenpenguin.co.uk

List of the Lost

Ezra, Nails, Harri, Justy. You'd dig hard and deep to excavate four names quite so unusual. Yet there they were and there they stood, sounding exactly like what they were. You would be offered a hearty shake of the javelin hand as expressions of possession of command from the four boys, each one fully developed into the blissful torment of their turnabout twentieth year – a pleasantly resolved marital union almost closed off in its camaraderie to the onlookers of the mookish greater world. Look at them now in their manful splendor and wonder how it is that they could possibly part this earth in dirt, as creased corpses, falling back as the skeletons that we already are, yet hidden behind musculature that will fall in time at life's finishing line. At such an unavoidable call they shall be minus all that they now have, here and today, at ease in the confidence of their physical weightlessness, united in athletic skill from which they beg no acquittal. Our four boys have no hidden disappointments, for they equally bear the gift of hip-to-ankle idolized speed, their bodies calmly narcissistic ass-to-the-grass instruments commingled to become, as they now knew they were, America's most sovereignly feared college relay team, with a unity that could send shivers through any braying jackass who might be fool enough to doubt them. The race begins and their bodies reply in relay, constantly responsible and on each other's watch; four bodies of one heart, never forgetting themselves as being one single reflection. Imperishable, they train insatiably; companions in pleasure and passionate in sentiments, they are the living picture of the desired physique and the voluntary affection amongst friends that survives time. Beyond each other and their will to run, they seek no other distraction. People magnetically attract others with similar weaknesses, as marriage rings the bell for the servile in hiding. Ezra, Nails, Harri and Justy performed marital duties as joined by strengths, but not weaknesses, and this crowned their lives. They each saw the desirable object within each other, and combined, they had no cause to justify one second of their contract. It may be quite true that we unwisely reduce others in order to make them ours, yet here was a foursome to whom no outward event could dent flesh or expression. It should be said that they were indeed contracting parties, since their combined aim was to dispose of every other half-mile relay team on any known college campus across the land, and this they must do, biological chance providing all the damn-straight confirmation that they would ever need. It is certainly something to dwell excitedly within a body that fully and proudly shows whatever the person is, since we all, for the most part, struggle in haunted fashion, unaware of ourselves as flesh, looking at a future that does not show promise, or back at a past that couldn't provide any, and permanently petrified at passing through without ever having lived. Undeveloped at twenty years, indecent thoughts at thirty years, the insoluble forty points to psychosomatic fifty, when moral inhibitions begin to laugh at the thought of further hope. The years pass as quickly as the sentence that describes their speed, yet you cannot believe it until you very suddenly look behind you and see a space once relied upon as being the future. Age sets its own terms, with its growing servitude catching that haunted reflection – one of no distinction because your frown now belongs to time. The wide-eyed girls were many, offering their conscious will as the running boys turned into overlords – strangers to the crowd yet well known in its imagination as the erotic reality of the deltoid deities who have no inhibitions in bodies fully occupied and enjoyed. The crowds look on with a lascivious dependency that a knife to the throat would never force them to admit. In servitude is the watcher, asking of the do-er that he assumes all aspects of the watcher's desire. The body is a thing only, of which we all irrationally fear … how to control, how to control … that which controls us. Heatedly the four gather daily, minus boos and taboos, free of the prohibitions that dishonor us all should we dare remark upon each other's physical good fortune (and lucky are those who might be remarked upon). We simply are not allowed to say. We employ sexual indifference as we gather in groups, schooled, as we are, against eroticisms, and any sudden desire registers as tension should our over-trained prejudices nap whilst our constitutional frigidity catches us looking – or, even worse, allowing ourselves to be looked at. Did you ever compliment a friend, a mere friend, on the directed desire of their eyes? Of course you didn't. Or on their sexually agreeable smile? Of course you wouldn't. Or on their hands – whose touch certainly does something as the waft of their passing being triggers unsuspecting impulses within unsuspecting you?

The will to find all of these motions in others runs strong in our being, yet we must only ever observe without acting, and even the very words that are in themselves a form of action ... must never be said. Day after day, year after year, we observe without operating, whilst the fact that we are only allowed to observe makes the will run and rise all the stronger. Worth is derived from approval, yet we discount the importance of our will to appreciate others because it is said to be a nothingness, or unwanted, or dangerously unsuspected. Yet, if I feel it, so must you, for it is you who made me feel so. Otherwise what is it that is 'there' for either of us to catch? Electrons from me need electrons from you in order to become electrons. Yet, there they are, and still you say nothing whilst always knowing. Look at the blue of the sky and tell me why you held back. Did you think there would one day be a bluer sky and a better hour? What did you think before you were aware?

Our four favored athletes have the task of relaying in relay and can therefore knock aside bothersome border boundaries as they guard each other's bodies as if all amounted to just the one. Their success depends upon the communal goal, the spring in eight legs, the combined methodology of four minds, and the maintained perfection of four physical frames; four wheels of the one machine. It is not possible to have any purpose other than the solvent fixity of openness and sharing. They contemplate each other's nature and structure, but not as a grasp on the sensual since, amongst other thoughts, there is a job to be done – a job almost as old as reading, one which fades faster than it blooms, batting away the decline that rots in life, a decline that must always win no matter how much you jog yourself into a headspin. Second by second the body is ponderable, ponderable, ponderable in any reflective surface.

In a pleasing suburb of the city of Boston, with its splendiferous stockbroker hamlets and bedroom communities of wide, tree-lined streets and pleasing market-town urbanization, the life-sized-puppet features of Mr Rims glare his magnified-fish countenance. As the boys' training coach, his briefing-guru gestures might seem to warrant large pinches of salt, for he provides entertainment in amongst the bootcamp intolerance of his sharpening-up chalk talk. He is easy fun, but with a resounding thud in his go-for-the-throat launching attack he mocks the boys as pudgy girls, and he assures them that whatever they do shall never get in the way of proper sprinters.

"It would be nice if you took yourselves seriously once in a while," he tells the boys as their punishing daily dozen drops each to the ground as if unable to do anything right. *"But then, we don't want to seem too pleased with ourselves,"* he mumbles whilst looking away, *"ambition exceeding grasp, and all of that."*

The boys of summer glare almost hatefully at the Sunday track, and the tryouts begin once more. Ezra is the lead-off man – twitch, twitch, twitching that all is in place; spikes, toes, elasticated waistband, everything comfortably arranged at the groin, and clear vision ahead with the right grip on the baton – firm, yet ready to loosen. Mr Rims' starting-pistol jumps in his hand as it fires, and the other hand clicks a shiny stopwatch as Ezra takes flight, all schoolboy soul passing perfectly to do-or-die Nails, licked into shape to hand over to Harri, whose big-leaguer grit finds anchorman Justy – the bull of the woods whose shafts of speed leave sparks across the finishing line. Huffing and breathless they then gather, facing Mr Rims for confirmation of something.

"Funeral pace," Rims chews, feigning disinterest. *"I could've walked in the time you took to run."* This isn't true, of course, but such sorry-butt putdowns are thought to sharpen self-respect. *"OK, so you're now warmed up,"* the coach croaks, even though two get-out-and-push hours have already dragged by. In the heat and the heart of the moment it is all never good enough, and the team ache for rest whilst wanting to perfect. Their dependency upon Mr Rims' glib jib annoys their spirits whilst also directing, as he repeatedly mumbo jumbo's his muttering mantra of *"get your head into the game".* A game it isn't, but with some muttonhead meaning such words find reason. There is no poetry in this military exercise, and yet it is understandable to cry with gratitude when it all goes well. All dietary modifications made, it becomes a sign of success when the boys feel too exhausted to sleep, but they are short sprinters and not tested for endurance, and so directed are they towards success that they can now only accept praise from those least likely to give it. Anything else is motherly encouragement – which will not do in the meathead world of savage sport. Light rain taps their faces like uncommitted kisses as early evening rush hour begins to hum from beyond the training ground. There is still no contentment from quibbling Rims, logic-chopping his way across every speedboat team attempt. Rims is only alarming if you are afraid of him, which the boys are not, but nonetheless there he is – a human speedometer whose insults facilitate and demolish the spirit in equal measure … *"My*

grandmaw moves faster than that," he drones with standard banality, *"may Satan ... rest her soul."* Stretching and high-kick exercises hone up on the scratch-gravel, and the fastidious-ness shows a spit-and-polish tone on these days that seem like nothing yet might have great meaning in years to come ... these months that gleefully suck the life out of your prime even though you think it must surely be far too early in life's story for reflected light to take root. None can be patient enough to let life take its course as the years creep upon us like energy thieves, and to be twenty years old has no vague importance to those who find themselves in such infancy, for there is time a-plenty to waste, and indeed to enjoy wasting. Closing the day, Mr Rims now talks to the boys almost as if they were proper people, and this change in tone signals the dying day, for Rims is homesick for the success that only the boys' can bring to him. This is a darker than usual April, with a major competition too close to jest about as June approaches like a meteorite in this year of 1975, so lavish with promise, so sadistic in demand. Only at the risk of their lives could the boys ever relax, and with never a moment's cease-fire they shall die with their spikes on. Justy slaps his leg muscles and Ezra jogs on the spot whilst lifting his knees comically high. Nails twists his upper torso as the lower body remains statue still, his hands on his hips, and Harri seeks some applause for his impressive one-armed push-ups. The boys are indeed licked into shape and ready to jockey and scramble even the feared fratern-ities of Lakeview and Bennington, from where rumors of hellion gazelles have taken the wind out of a nation's sails. The hand-off, here in God's own Boston, has been so skil-fully mastered that the most difficult task ahead will be

7

shaking hands and kissing babies – the names of our track-sters called out to, yet unanswered, as bleacher observers rise to their feet and shout to our boys as if believing in nothing else. Easy victories do not await, but just rewards seem like a tasty cakewalk, a wrapped-up walkover, so neat and ready to breast the tape. They remind us all of what it is to be living, just as they might show you that you *are not*, but their natural joys can prevent us from dwelling on our own private failings. As innocent as water, as fueled as a bursting tank, their drunken rapture is found in their natural selves, ready to be televised and then pressed for their secrets like an imperious political dynasty. The athlete is very alone and must control every outcome, knowing how an unforeseen blunder shall be judged as the beginning of the end – or, even worse, the end of the beginning. You might let others down when such a move is the opposite of your intentions, and the shifting nature of luck leaves you privately howling.

There are days of genuinely poor visibility when your sorry best is the most you can do, whereas a dry and radi-ant day expects more from you and is ready to catch you victimized by excuses. Well, either you can run or you can't, and no eloquent apologies are acceptable substitutes for hair-raising action. Somewhere alone within the hole of the soul it is known that the page is already turning, and the future is a time when you will only watch. Fully present in today, you will make the most of yourself as you dig deep to bring out whatever will save you, for isn't it true that we have within us everything that we seek outside, from others? Ah, the competitive spirit which would endanger its own soul if it accepted less. It is never enough to assume that it will right itself when your name is called, and you twist within such a burden of responsibility so that the concentration prods like a long-term agony. It is a power that needs more power – and here and now, in this world but not the next. The thrill is not the race, but the point at which the race successfully ends, for there are no consolations to be had at third or fourth place – your brake lights evidently mysteriously snipped. By chance, our teamsters are four wind-shot greyhounds, and nature bestowed as much, as each makes the same deadly quicksilver strike in his different way. Their jet-plane speed and their blue-darter health are fully equated with natural virtue, and once they step on the gas or flatten the grass nothing else in life has class. Backward flips motion without any thought; it is just there, always, without cautious planning. Their surf-board bodies came genetically, as fat fanatics gaze on depressively. Perfectionism is what few possess as raw instinct, and you might work as hard as you wish yet find yourself still remaining your true Sara Lee podgy slug. Vanilla runners such as Ezra and Nails have never known chemical adventures – their Hispanic backgrounds somehow unimpressed with letting the air out of optimism – whereas pale-faced Justy and Harri were briefly blue-eyed and round-eyed devils who very quickly found their way back before any serious habits and hooks took the last of their luck or led them knuckle to knuckle with the machete of justice. All of that doesn't matter now, because June looms with the most important day they shall ever have as a team, when national television cameras document a major track defeat for boneless Bennington and gassed Lakeview, our Priorswood tetrad repaid with paradise for all of their hard work. Nails didn't care too much about what he did in life as long as he did something well, scarred as he was by his scrappy social background of unrelenting parental disapproval, of the untouchable question of religion's fatal grip, of hate and hurt persistently bruising a harmless heart, whereas Justy had fared better in a rambling house full of upper-hand sisters (although they had always been *they*, whilst he would always be *other* due to whitewashed gender divides and separations that appeared to crop up hourly, and just occasionally with some meaning). Divine love had blessed Ezra, who had always won due to his physical and facial features – an amorously fixed gaze so sensually in place and all-American Alien strong that it would be commented upon time and again as if it were all he'd ever need. Nails had no family as such, having been abandoned and then discovered by a set of adoptive parents, whose methods of love were far too harsh to benefit the boy. Thus he assured himself that he was indeed as hard as nails, since life had insisted upon as much. He, too, had always been a desired one beyond the gloomy lair of the family home, and it would be forever assumed that his sharpened body accurately reflected his needs – which it did not; but at the same time he denied no bouquets that flew his way, and many there were. Touch came second to watching, though, and this troubled him without his understanding why, even though such shame was easily readable in a modern American society that worked very hard to keep sex out of commission. At a standstill, sexual experience became the one thing that most young people thought about, usually with worried countenance, and soon they would grow to fear it and learn to suppress it without finding out anything new about it – or about themselves in relation to it. If it worked it must only work one way ... like most things in life. Parents approved only of sex within marriage, which also served as the ultimate threat to trying anything else with others. Conversely, Harri (a boy alone with his mother) and Justy opted for a certain less-educated mimicry, since they were romantically unsuccessful yet managed to keep such a truth unsaid, and simply made the most of what little they knew.

Sex was always there – everywhere photographically, in print, in film, so expansively thought about that almost nothing more could need to be said about it ... yet ... so difficult to obtain, not because of the appearances of Justy and Harri, but because of the atomic supremacy in the family values of their upbringing which, of course, circumscribed the sons' freedom to fly, since a certain sexlessness kept the grown child tied to the family, even if the impossibly constricted demands could very easily lead to a form of sexual cremation for the young child. The parental mind would allow the child time to develop political views, but there would certainly be no question of allowing the child time to choose its preferred religion, and, even more importantly, the grand assumption that all children are extensively heterosexually resolved at birth whipped a demented torment across the many who were not. Whether physical maneuvers were difficult or easy (and it is usually one or the other, and for eternity), our foursome found in each other a generosity of spirit and determination that all other circumstances seemed blind to. Each would make up for the other's loss – so firmly they took their friendship into their own hands, and around it went. Only Ezra worried that four males had found each other to be so emotionally indispensable to one another, yet he could not argue in favor of a better situation. In fading light he had met Eliza – the similarity of their names! … that e and that z! – and she provided enough initial silence for Ezra to fill as he'd wish, even if her all-show-and-no-go banished Ezra's warmness for her formness to initially go its full distance. In such circumstances Ezra had only ever known sunlight, his thigh-blaster trophies easily acquired as he handled the female structure with an expertise that almost suggested aloofness – so speedily he knew, so speedily he unclasped, so confident his aim, like banking deposits.

"What are you doing tonight?" he asked Eliza.

"Seeing you," she felt assured.

"That is the correct answer. Well done." Ezra had been a beacon of light to so many females as there they lay, under the male, with nothing to lose. Up and into his eyes they looked, finding an almost primitively embarrassing meaning, finding that they finally had a name, and Ezra alone taught them to see themselves through their lovers' eyes. It wasn't easy, and the gift worked both ways, of course, but it did different things to different hearts. And why shouldn't it? Sameness meant that nothing moves on. Occupied by Ezra, the girl-woman somehow enjoyed the sensation of feeling oily and disgusting, and as Ezra flashed his 'no biting' smile, he playfully bit her ear hard enough to hurt yet not hurtful enough to matter. It is rough with the boys, as Eliza will find, just as it is boring with the considerate gentlemen. For his part, Ezra was appreciative,

but would never be the dazed underling, and neither would he ever be cheap enough to be cruel. Eliza, though, had caught him unawares, because although she awakened him, full gratification would not be quite so prompt. Of similar height (should these things matter), they amused each other daily with dilly-dally and doo-lally repartee, the kind which neither would accept from others.

"I have an old soul," begins Eliza.

"I am a model of healthy humanity," chops Ezra.

"Friendship is a waste of time," lobs Eliza.

"I dream of a booze-infused orgy," shoots Ezra.

*"I **am** a booze-infused orgy,"* is Eliza's reverse-twist.

"I have erotic curiosities," topspins Ezra.

"I can take life as it is and leave it at that," backhands Eliza.

"I slow down to inspect traffic accidents at the risk of causing another," lies Ezra.

"You mustn't keep asking yourself why you feel what you feel," is Eliza's dropshot.

"I am a flawless triumph!"

"I am a floored triumph!"

"I take myself very seriously," is Ezra's sudden half-volley.

"... therefore I do not need to ..." serves Eliza.

"I am a puzzle,"

"I, a solution,"

"I am flimsy,"

"I am whimsy," the ground strokes went on, leading nowhere, for the tiebreak was truced and the play-and-serve love match was an even double.

"I am the perfect fiancée," leaned in Eliza.

"I am the perfect fiasco," advanced Ezra, headmanning a drop pass. Furiously paced, this private nonsense went on

until at least one face cracked, not because any of the puck-handled dribble had been funny in the least, but because, well, what it must be to be in love.

At the ivy halls in dreamy central Beantown, the quartet warmed up beneath the contemptuous giant shadow of Priorswood, with its tower aloft like a snooty nose of supremacy, its historic standing being reason enough to glare down with full repulsion at the deformed modern world. Sprinklers on the football field and sunlight flooding The Great Library wheezed a privileged blow of warm air across the absorbed and collected students of intense expressions and processed formulations clanking about inside their spaghetti heads – so small and lost are they, so petty their actual blood-and-guts experience, yet oh so very ripe for clever positions within the judiciary or the media, and with their narrow historical views the students will become unbreakable in their steely assurances, and whatever the unreliable and self-serving shit story history books have left out does not matter, as long as their own life happens as designed, for it is all and absolutely only about money. Social consciousness and abnormal pre-eminence certainly take their little place at Priorswood, whilst naked life is elsewhere, and is irrelevant when pitted against the literary pretensions and superiority complex of social position. The catatonic magpies are called to and they line up, and the theorists theorize without ever getting their feet wet. Ezra whispers in warning to the other three. *"It's here,"* he says, as Mr Rims approaches. *"Did he really part with money for that shirt?"* murmured Justy.

"He found it on a bus," smiled Nails.

"He found it down the back of a couch," added Justy.

"I heard exactly what you just said," came Mr Rims, jejune jesting (having heard nothing), and well aware of his clichéd self. *"Even worse, I saw that last track attempt and I wonder what exactly you'd call it. Performance art ... Community Theater? It's anybody's guess, of course. I at least had the benefit of watching you from the window and no closer. That's all that can be said in your favor."*

"We were just practicing," smiled the Ezra of goodness.

"Evidently," sniffed Mr Rims. *"Now, as you know, complaining is all I have left in life, but I like to think I still have my finger firmly up the pulse when it comes to choosing track teams. You let my good name down and I'll probably kill you, and I'll gleefully assure the police that your sudden death was not an accident. This day is all about discipline, exercise, practice, preparation, conditioning ... all the things that you lack."*

"We're on it," affirmed Harri.

"You're certainly on something," rocketed back Rims. *"Now. You do know the date, the month and the year that we are currently in?"*

The foursome didn't bother to answer or even to nod as this teasing twitter played out its daily dozen. Hamstring and tendon yakkety-yak backchats and gabs as the afternoon sun loses its edge and gentle music yawns across the lawns. There is shrill laughter from an open window, so ditzily unreal, and Ezra thinks of Eliza as she was – in a simple dress with a low neckline and no sleeves.

"I'm definitely having a baby," she had said. Flustered, Ezra paused and fumbled, asking her to repeat what she had just said as Eliza marvelled at the richness of his gullibility.

"In Dutch or English?" she snapped with a scowl of power. She then explained that the baby was not currently within, but that the wish would one day certainly be fulfilled. *"I'm not saying by you – necessarily. I'm just saying that … eventually … should I find myself in the Holy City … living in a friendly room with books, then I'd let myself go to one of the savage hordes … he of strong jawline and fierce gentleness … and hey presto … the process … such as has ever been the way."*

"The pro-cess?" stammered Ezra, looking all of ten very confused years of age.

"Oh, I see … linguistic expertise …" she has faltered. *"Yes, that sounds like something I didn't mean at all. Life takes the strangest turns, and I'm not saying that you, pumpkin of my pumping heart, do not strike me as the perfect father … but we must just be … and not rely, otherwise I see myself crushed and bewildered and unable to get up again."* Eliza enjoyed overweening confidence at such times as these, because she knew she could inflame the dim light of Ezra's confusion which, in turn, re-shaped his face to an appealingly shy appeal for peace and mercy. Eliza was now on top with Ezra being entered with as much professional aggression as deemed necessary. Incitement to mayhem.

There is a querulous pause. *"Ezra,"* she now began with softened tone, *"should I leave my husband and come and live with you?"* This form of play is coy bait, since Eliza does not – and has never had – a husband, but much of Eliza's jabs would not depend upon rational justifications for both were in that state known as love, when even the defensive fencing sends a sexual shiver.

"Have you ever considered a wordless existence? You'd fare far better," Ezra now joins in, and both relax.

"*Yes, I have considered a wordless existence ... since words could never be accurately found to describe all of ... this,*" she waves a hand out in quite stately sweep ... but at nothing.

"*You were very smart, Eliza. But something dashed your brains out at some point. Do you understand me at all?*"

"*Yes, I do, but only at all. Nowhere else, and I am not vulnerable to offense because of, well, let's just describe it as an abnormally solid wall of love for you. Undeserved at times, perhaps, but I'm immune to argument on the subject, and what a joy to be able to finally say these words for the first time ... catching your breath as you sigh ... finally in the living world. But we need each other in order for us both to be good, and to hold on to a certain unshakeable belief without reason.*"

"*There are certain things which are best not to mess around with. Human thoughts, for example, haha. But, look, you are my heart. You save me every single day from ... absolute boredom. This is how I know I ... pause ... love you.*"

"*You haven't finished the sentence,*" clips in Eliza; "*the bit where we move in together is missing ... and the other frazzled issue of my new life and, my, my how your expressions alone reveal your deepest insights ... or at least they give me mine, should I say? Or are our lives too ordinary to be worth yammering about?*"

"*What would your mother say if you said 'I'm pregnant and I'm leaving home'?*" asked Ezra.

"*If I told her you were pregnant and leaving home I think she'd be quite pop-eyed ... should the gin allow.*"

"**Is** *that clear, Ezra?*" This voice now belonged to Mr Rims, breaking into Ezra's dream, the danger signal that reality must always be. Ezra realized that he had not listened to anything at all said by Mr Rims, or by anyone else, as all five squatted on the grassy green of Priorswood propriety. A grin broke across Ezra's face, as if this alone could assure Rims.

"Jesus, you're a devil," rounded off Rims. And that was that.

The boys break it open on the track, but Harri tanks at third base and bolts into a header. It's a poor show under tension.

*"**Muzzle**-head!"* shouts Rims … *"infidel!"* he clips on, and all are quietly embarrassed.

With just over a month to go before the competition where middle- and long-distance events shape lives forever, our foursome pack life's inessential essentials in migration for a holistic fortnight at a sportsman's haven known as Natura, a no-nonsense collegiate retreat where countrywide affiliations commune in one hearty scholastic clash, where a single-track road led to the hidden pavilion of an abandoned plantation shadowed by giant dawn redwoods five meters in girth; where deadly dale led to stumpery woods, and slippery stepping stones crisscrossed over dangerously racing rapid rivers. Natura's facilities were not necessarily more useful than those at Priorswood, but the colonization of contenders cramped within shared living quarters brought the critically serious within competitive towel-whacking distance of those whom they'd zealously oppose in combat on that final commercialized Pillsbury Doughboy-soaked televised day. This tested preparedness and authority and overall composition, weeding out wet-knickered nerves and any lingering sensitivities. In fact, our team converged at Natura without making any exchanges whatsoever with the other mariner athletes, thus the intensification of such a move ultimately felt lost on the unit. Woodland surrounds of cud-chewing laziness wrapped Natura in a soon-to-be-shorn lamb's warmth and protection, here, where humans are allowed to feel almost as dignified as nature, and where an immediate harmony with silence and beauty (which most of us have learned to live without) embraced the boys as a pictorial love affair began. The city peasantry is ineffectual here, and they will call it wilderness whilst not knowing the meaning of such a word, yet somehow acknowledging the moral superiority of land untrammeled by the flapping mediocrities that make up the simple-minded majority. These woods are an eternal ocean, familiar to you only from television; they are gamely danger-ous or overripe with majesty depending upon your surging urgings to give an opinion. Nature always waits in the wings and the winds, ready to pounce with all of its power just at that sloppily contented hour when you foolishly assume it to be plainly tired out. Narcissistic humans do their quite pathetic best to kill nature off, oblivious to their self-reliance on its upkeep, yet nature will only take so much bureaucratic bullying before it snaps a deadly snap – for it does not need your approval, your organized banditry, your prepubescent social laws, your trades of cheapening commerce, your militant preachment, your apologies or blind belief of superiority … as if a presidential seat gives you an intolerable presumption of dominance over this earth's terrain! Watch, wait and listen, and soon you'll be bitten. Natura indeed means *mother nature*, and here she is all around you, as you stand shyly abandoned, denying that what was said was ever intended. Early evening has our hounds in leisurely stroll through deep-dell woodland where oxygen almost chokes you with its purity, for there are no chunky human discontents fanatically generating their defective habits. Animals do not pollute, do not need a god in order to be good, and live in organized societies of reciprocal altruism. Animals do not need money, and they will even feed the subordinates within their kin. Humans, on the other hand, live entirely upon repayment of favors given, and on a costly demonstration of superiority that thrives on divine punishment. New air rolls into the city in order to save it, yet it is defiled by the smack and shuffle of everyday destruction of Neanderthals posing as modernities, causing nothing more serious than life simply needing to do its part. Our speed merchants do what we all do in the stimulating silence of woodland of mature oak trees and wingnut trees: they throw back their heads and they squint to the tallest point of the tallest evergreen, and then they walk slowly, with mouths agape, yew cones underfoot in wild flower meadow. Yet what makes wild bluebells wild? And could they ever be tamed? Is a caged animal no longer wildlife? Or is it in fact wilder still, due to its incarceration? Marshy montezuma pines line the pathway through the woods, and deer are here – knowing enough about the evils of the human spirit to keep well hidden, for the human race is *anything but humane*. They have created the hell of the slaughterhouse, aflame and far more perverted in sickness than anything apparently designed by Satan. Ah, yes, the human race: impinging and threatening with every gleeful twist of the branding iron.

Whilst the city demands that we jaunt instead of stroll, slaves to the hands of the clock, the clock, the clock (even though a moochie traipse might be all that's required of you), this pathway through the woods makes no such demands. You walk as you please, amongst yew, lime and maple marsh, none of which fear time as pathetically imperialist you do. With the howl of a dog, Nails dances through the woods, happiness in high gear.

"It's on ice! It's on ice!" he shouts, and nature's space returns an impressive echo. The others know what he means, and are even dismayingly amused by his orgiastic war dance. Nails has no doubt whatsoever that the ultimate trophy awaits at the upcoming barnburners competition, as late bird-song, here, in the pine-coned hollow, is heard as ever it has been, undisturbed since the original and native Americans (now blanketed and blue-penciled out of his-story and her-story) first sprayed their pioneer's mark on a country that really wasn't ever kind to its own people. Of the white race no explanation is necessary because expectations are so low. Nails rocks along in mock fun-house mirror buffoonery, and no one knows why, and it hardly matters. Ezra thinks of Eliza, and he wonders if she thinks of how he thinks of her.

"... and if we fail, we shall fail magnificently!" lords Justy, and with this he hurls his wristwatch into the shrubbery as he shouts, *"I refuse to be a slave! I refuse to be a spectator! This body is decorative art! I delight in my own magnificence! Why shouldn't I? War is an old, shitty business! I am young! The nuclear arms race is a mass mental illness! Nuclear physicists are highly paid serial kill-ers! All they can think of is cremation. Why aren't they all on Death Row? I am alive! I will not be destroyed by regulations!"* The dance goes on.

"Yes, very good, stop it now, please, or I'll split your head," says Harri, flatly.

Curled and hidden amongst the flora and fauna that run

alongside a boundary-line bridle path, a small and crumpled figure is doing his best to stand upright amongst primrose and violets. Soundlessly the boys freeze as five sets of eyes assess each other. Nobody speaks. No civilized description could bring to life an outlined sketch of the elderly imp swaying like a nightmarish object of hardbitten brutality, with his torn overcoat blacker than death and his face lined and marked with the sorriest scars – dispossessed, dehumanized and insidious, this intimidating ding-a-ling wreck is at the end of everything, and possibly wanting the end sooner rather than later. The hunched hobo has no hair, his skin a dish of human dirt, his bearing having already drifted into the final chapter as if it were death. His voice suddenly spoke, as if half-strangled in his own throat. From the swill-bucket mouth came breath that could kill off a team of horses, and hands like withered leaves made fumbling motions as an occultist drone of despair dripped from his chipped and chapped lips.

"Well, none of youze is black, so I suppose you won't kill me," he starts. The human sickbed steps closer, a stench of stale medication vaporizing from his gaseous and perished clothing, to which evidently cling bits of herb garden. A pitiful vision of life's loneliness, his timid steps suggest a man pushed past his limit and now ready to feud with his own grave. His cataracts mist the pain, but the agonized mouth knows that only midnight is ahead, with no further chance of recovery from enforced oblivion. The voice speaks with the tone of struggle, passive goodwill, yet sorrowfully nowhere, neither myth nor fiction. Only so much despair can be survived before the mind finally caves in. Trapped in his clothes, trapped in his history – the history

that created him, and he is here, one of the lowest of the lower animals. He is now his total outcome, the inevitable moral and physical defeat, changeless in its ignominy.

"I generally can't stand young people … taking drugs for the good of the country … how does that help? Taking chemicals to experience natural happiness? Everyone has something to hide, of course, and power is all very well, but nobody's powerful enough to leave this world alive, haha. Do the rich go to a richer heaven? Do kings and queens go to a special royal heaven? Haha, I don't think so. But why not, if they're as royal as they say they are? But if a cop places his hands on me I will do my level best to kill him, I really will. I am nothing and I have nothing but I hate the cops because I know them and I know what they are. There is no safety and nobody cares about you, make no mistake about that. The cops, even, yes, my very country-men, are my biggest enemy – only schoolyard shitheads join the police machine, you've noticed, I'm sure. Shake your head as you will, but while I still have my senses … I've seen some beautiful houses, not far, quite near, and they look like what you'd call success … y'know, that senseless trance of absolute boredom … but is it success? I don't know because I'm not the one living inside those houses and I'm not the one who pays for them, so I don't know if the word 'success' is even applicable because it could be sheer hell inside those dark-hearted walls for all I know, and I must tell you that the people down there don't look too happy to me … all them frozen postures and changeless actions … impossibly restricted by their own wealth. Their tax money funds atomic testing grounds in Nevada. They blow up live pigs imagining them to be Muslims. Affecting, isn't it? And through it all they talk of God, as all war-mongerers do. I see the sun shining on the water and a shock of joy rips through me like it's the most true and pure pleasure that life can ever give you. Shake your head as you will, but while I still have my senses. Most things end and you

23

don't even remember them. Most **people** end and you don't even remember them, like my wife, if you want an instance. I'll give you an instance. She lost her mind and was gently led away to die – don't ask me where to because I didn't care enough to ask. I'd had no education, no proper job, and being on state aid was just a blatant way of doing nothing – I knew that. My wife just sat there. I didn't even know her and I was expected to feed and clothe her for the rest of her life, and all because ... of what? Because she allowed me access. I couldn't even feed and clothe myself! And I asked for nothing! She just sat there, anyway, in her bed-chamber of horrors, exiled, as if she'd been in a fire or something, as if she'd lost her lower body in the war and as if nothing could possibly be expected of her because she was the woman. Proceed carefully because marriage is just a ... suffocation ... your life doesn't belong to you. Shake your head as you will, but while I still have my senses. Well, I lost and that's that. Not that I wish to press the point. I was four years too young, I really was, and my mind keeps wandering back to that desolate time, it really does. Well, the dead are dead. You can't go through life knowing who you'll fall in love with, and I want no god judging me for whatever I ... think, never mind do! When I was first married I didn't realize that you couldn't do the intimate physical bit unless you felt confident about it, otherwise it just couldn't work. I didn't like that fact, but it was a fact nonetheless. Anyway, I discovered I was useless and then I didn't have a choice, and once you've faced the mocking nature of making love badly then you can never get free of it. But if I hadn't been so afraid I would have found out more about it, and wouldn't I have been happier so? A girl laughed at me when we were both thirteen years old, and that widening mouth of laughter, as dumb and sterile as it was, the vicious disdain because I couldn't measure up ... but it was the **way** she laughed ... the way **she** laughed ... the way she **laughed** ... with all that hair like something pulled out of a

*microwave ... like something you'd twirl on a stick ... it stayed with
me forever, and it triggered my dislike of all women, or, my embarrassment at women. I'd known a boy from over the back, and I'd
stand on tip-toe to watch him every day at four o'clock* [now his
eyes became greedy], *not knowing why at first. I'd wait to the
point of excited tears. The patience I gave! And I was thirteen to his
sixteen! You'd laugh or cry! I'd shake his arm off – but, ah, the
demands of other people, other people, other people, other people, other
people ... but what about me, and what I felt? What makes my
feelings so ... impossible to satisfy? And if they're impossible to
satisfy then ... why are they there ... in God's image! Who says I'm
faulty? No one dies any differently to anyone else. It's all the same
passage. Which of us doesn't die? And if someone soothes my hurts,
what does it matter to those who aren't involved? Sexual morality is
just an unpleasant excuse to snoop into other people's lives – bored
as you must be with your own. They said my emotions were unusual,
but they weren't unusual enough for there not to be laws against them,
so they must have been quite common, in fact, and not unusual at all.
He was a good whistler, and that's a sign of a very contented mind,
isn't it? I know people don't walk along and whistle any more, but
they did then, you see, each hand in each pocket. I knew I need only
wait, because it roared out of me – louder than any roar I'd roared!
And we're meant to be whatever we are, otherwise we wouldn't have
been made to be whatever we are. I can't be entirely wrong. My wife,
you see, was just a mouth ... just a mouth and nothing else ... she
was just about better than nothing ... although, on reflection ... She
yawned from morning till night even though she wasn't tired. I never
knew love – equal love – and I thought the consolation of physical
contact would ... well, lust has nothing to do with all of the other
emotions ... it's a separate emotion in itself. I found that, anyway.
Bless me, yes. In any case, my wife rambled like a martyr and we'd*

25

only been two months married, but she wasn't happy and I told her she was contaminated and I now don't think she was, but I couldn't think of anything else to say, and neither of us could imagine living and not being unhappy, but we were too shy to talk to doctors or anything like that because we couldn't imagine anyone being interested in our problems. It wasn't a settled home ... padlocks, fifty sets of keys, and we only had four rooms in total. I had full cause to grieve, and there were no possibilities to make progress, because you were kept where you were – by the state – shoved further and further and further down by a mass of laws that I'd never consented to in the first place. Once it had all ended and the homeless shelter had told me to go away, then the welfare kitchen reported me to the police. I mean, what do the police know? They don't live in the slums ... Judges don't live in the ghetto ... they are exclusively verbal beings. What can they understand about the way life moves? They have no precise meaning. What makes them royal? What makes anyone royal? Being in possession of a squad of tanks? Would judges even recognize dog shit if ever they saw it? Their interests are not the same as ours, so what gives them the right to judge us? They don't understand the houses we live in, or why we persist. They're scared to death of the underprivileged ... whose powerlessness gives them an almighty power. Judges live in secrecy, don't they, because they've done so much harm to society ... they have to hide like criminals on the run. I've never seen the Chief of Police breaking bread with the bag people, no, no, no. The police think it's OK to shoot anyone as long as control is the outcome, which is just like saying it's OK to bomb foreign countries if it means we get to control them. How did that ever become constitutional? The game is rigged! Like there's nothing on earth but control! And control can never be wrong! And the cops! They know very well what they do to innocent people, and they don't want it done back to them! Anyway, you're all next. The military! ... dreaming up new ways to wipe out entire populations. How evil could any human mind possibly be? Shake your head as you will. Do you think I was always seventy-five years old? Bless me, no. Being this old is new to me. This is why I can't take to young people. They think the elderly have been elderly for years and years, but we haven't, we've just turned old from being young – and all we know about is being young! You'd laugh if I said I was no different to you – but it's true. My mind is twenty-one. I can't recognize the body I have now ... because it isn't mine ... I'm new at being old. I ran like a frightened gazelle, and I'd spring like a poked cobra, but you can't stay that way forever, and I can't talk about it enough. Yet what am I left with? My wife and I had nothing in common, and that's what brought us together! We were meant for one another 'cos we were both useless! She said she was dying from sexual neglect – but she was lucky because I didn't even know there was any other way to feel. Well, I knew it as a marketing ploy, or from the television ... as profitable as war. Did you know that every government needs *a war in order to balance the books? Did you know that every government* **loves** *a war?* **Woo-hoo!** *'Our hearts go out to the families of the heroes' ... well, stop sending them out to futile death, then. Those boys are so heroic that no one can be bothered to mention their names.* **Woo-hoo!** *You chase it every single day of your life until its mocking nature all but destroys you, and I can't talk about it enough, yet we laugh at small children who still believe in the Tooth Fairy – but we do, too! Until the day we die! I can't talk about it enough. I said, I can't talk about it enough. Have you seen much action yourself?"* He now, suddenly, moves too close to Ezra, as if heaving into place.

"Have you? Have you seen much action? Come before me and know me, Tommy ..."

The punching-bag face is now stiff with dirt, and the oily hands wring with pulpy sweat as his eyes melt into Ezra, who is now standing astride – as if balanced for attack, or ready to be swabbed down by hand. Trouble comes unexpectedly by a lightning-fast pinch between Ezra's legs as the wretch leaps over the psychological and physical line only to be met by a ferocious neat-as-a-pin side-swipe to the right cheek bone, too tear-ass fast for the eye to track, and the anchor-weight school ring of Ezra's third finger left hand clips the temple of the wretch with such a knee-pumping dead-shot that the morgue-bound leper obediently slumped backwards on to a knoll of deadly nightshade, where the hard root of a knotted oak spiked through scalp and skull-bone with deadly thrust, smashing the cerebrum and bursting out blood from the sensory organs. Amongst the dead wood and the dead nettle, the cave-dweller was out of play; a lumpenprole dead weight within less than an instant, seventy-five years to reach such a jell-brained release … but to where, to where? And why must we believe that there is a next stage? Does our sanity depend upon it?

Harri placed the back of his right palm onto the man's exposed chest, kneeling before an outcast now fully cast out. *"I think this is his way of telling us he's dead."* He looks up to the standing three of frozen postures, to whom that final word had no logically given reality. As if blind to the present, all stood together in sour recognition, yielding to their own silence whilst glumly understanding the correct reasoning of Harri's words. It could only be Ezra who spoke first, with his proclamation of *"Dead!"* as both hands clasped each side of his face in shock at being just barely able to say that one word alone. The diagnosis was by now obvious enough not to need repeating. Little brown babblers darted in and around surrounding bushes, their

28

movements announcing the luck of new life still moving on. Instinctively the three dragged the body inches further into wrap-around heather and warm fawn, and there it would be hidden with very little undergrowth required to snuggle around what barely passed as human form. The sorry hayseed clump had worried its last, and now, oh so very quickly, its ordeal of insanity had ended, the woodhick sucked in by encircling and coddling blackness shaded by weeping willow, weeping ash, weeping beech and weeping life.

"Why did we do that?" asked Nails, struggling for breath and belief.

"Why nothing, let's tear-ass as fast as we can away from this … whatever it is, whatever it was," came Justy, suddenly the scoutmaster that he had never been. In times of strife, any leading voice will do; off-key though it might be, it belongs to a star of the first magnitude if it speaks the common aim of strong confidence. As if a starting-pistol had fired they scampered like scared rabbits taking off in a cloud, further into the woodland masterminding a birdlike swing to left and then right in unified swerve through the woebegone sticks like migratory geese following ancient winds; large chestnut and horse chestnut looked down laughing … through an old grotto rock garden fenced in by overgrown box hedges – loved by someone in 1920, now a mess of silver birch and cypress. With their natural speed it did not take long before a sharp westerly bend found them out of the woods and home-free into the clear coast of the safe-and-sound edge of a town where suddenly they were no different from those they walked amongst, and they methodically wondered if they had even been there

at all, with the wretch, in hollow's hell. Ezra's steely clip had indeed ended a life. How we endure our own feelings having done such an act is beyond our powers to reason, and perhaps all answers are in the particles of brain unused, yet once the hammer has fallen it is not a new reality at all, even if yesterday now feels like a lifetime ago; and even if moral action is not entirely well thought out it is powerfully instinctive nonetheless. The only shock for Ezra was the ease by which the wretch became vegetation, evolved from nothing and now returned – and by such a simple shot. There then came a troubling inner glow, one which sad-sack soldiers in combat must enjoy as they lovingly assist history books with their abysmal confidence game, motivated by their own faith yet beyond the power of their own awareness. The wretch had been unknown to Ezra and had, after all, instigated the provocation and outcome, so therefore any broad view of the situation might consider the solution with a certain moral certainty that would favor Ezra. Every moment in life takes its little place, and Ezra – so full of heart and soft to the eye against the subterranean dogface of our sickly fleshed goner – held a certain unsophistication if ever to be judged as a cold-blooded killer. The wretch, too, was a man, but had positioned himself so far away from obedient society that no one who mattered was close to him, or even knew him. Worm-chow for the crops, he was dead, dead, dead. The internal infrastructure was still closing down even though the unlovable heart had pumped its final tick, or possibly tock. For what earthly reason would anyone care? Why should anyone care now if they hadn't whilst his machinery continued to pump air within? Would there be a solitary fly-bait throughout the entire woodland that could fare any worse? The wretch was now cold meat with the thing he most loved: nothing. Had life continued he might have starved to death or been beaten up by the local rookies – both fair outcomes in the eyes of the yawningly law-bending law. His time had been called in mid-sentence and without one full second allowed for him to understand whatever it was that had befallen him, and time crowds in even if we think we have it under control.

Nails, Ezra, Justy and Harri felt off-center, but nothing more. All assumed joint responsibility, or at least equal understanding, and there would be no instinctive rush to isolate Ezra since all would have acted in precisely the same way had they, and not Ezra, been zeroed in upon, because most people come to the same moral conclusions when faced with awkward moral conundrums. The syphilis-itch of the hobo's grope would be enough to repulse the softest composure, and Ezra had no doubt that his automatic slug had been provoked, and no one who had not been present at the scene of the senicide could have any right to another view. Yes, there is judicial law, and, yes, there is natural law. Equally with the four their impulse was to acknowledge a death and to leave it alone. Something happens to the body and the corpse is whisked out of view, and your dignity urges you to move your thoughts onwards and elsewhere, knowing that the foul-smelling human corrosion had ventured too far. Urine-soaked, he could not possibly have imagined the intoxicated rash of his lips stuck to Ezra's face. We cradle each wish in preparation of it being fulfilled, and our feelings might be so bullishly strong that we cannot imagine the object of our lust being unimpressed by the sheer voltage and force of our needs (since it obviously impresses *us*). But life tends to be a cold-storage schlep of mediocrity at best, and amongst the snowed-under years our theories of love and lust are almost never practiced with the vim and vigor haven so brutally immovable from our stuck imaginations, even if their demand irrationally urges its force ahead of basic hunger and intelligence. This makes the human being a pitiful creature eternally occupied with *longing, longing, longing* – yet animals, at least (at most?), leap as large as life when ready to cloy in ecstasy. Humans, on the other hand, require novels, films, food, labor, plays, magazines, pornography and castles in Spain in order to substitute for the urgings of the loins – and, alarmingly, they accept those substitutes. Well, what choice?

By 8 p.m. the four boys were adequately distanced from the ever-stiffening stiff who was now lying in possibly his first ever repose of gentleness. Where he was now could not be worse than where he had been a few hours ago. You can't let go of everything, of course, and his shattered shell remained under bush, the mouth now fallen open as if attempting one last futile call for a mercy that had never previously been on offer. Every imaginable sign of desolation slid him away. A ghastly almost-eaten face, he had gone to such excessive lengths to survive, but this did not matter very much after all. He was dead and he simply must *stay* dead, flitting about in time and space, with perhaps only a few random photographs (of the tortured-family variety) somewhere to guarantee that he once *was*. No prayer or fireworks could undo his fate, and any lyric poetry in passing on or passing away was not reserved for his exit. Those random photographs, not treasured but stuffed away somewhere, gave conclusive testimony to his existence, when nothing else now could. Tomorrow will happen without him and tonight will not miss him, as storms gathered as they ought to under such circumstances. How he had lived had not been deemed difficult enough, and the God to whom he occasionally pleaded was, even now, no doubt still judging him, as if death could not be thought sufficient final pain and mockery in itself.

Four heavy hearts sat by a roadside bar with their straws like daggers chipping away at the crushed ice in their soft drinks. They had nothing to say yet they all knew. Sore-footed, they decided upon the long walk back to the barracks, all choosing to believe that the death of the wretch had not happened, yet at the same time they were in no rush to hear any bad news of discovery being broadcasted with spectator's high-pitched glee; news hounds so terribly appalled at the discovery of a body about whom no one cared whilst alive (and about whom no one *would* care should it suddenly rise from silence). Whilst the boys had agreed amongst themselves that the incident had not actually taken place, they would also not mention the night's events even quietly amongst themselves. What's done in the dark remains in the dark.

Nervous vitality would scour each of all emotional involvement or responsibility; that moment had gone, and they would now exercise an innocence with a talent as impressive as anything shown on track and field. The grandstand event ahead offered the promise of an American all-time best, a lifetime's achievement along with a victoriously swinging gold medal, and, for this, cold-blooded routine returned for the following two weeks as mental and physical preparation continued in top-dog Boston training clubs and a new spurt urged them into spirited mid-day sessions and a heavy heat stretched throughout the month of May. *"Yes,"* Mr Rims drawled a drawn-out sigh, *"you've caught the scent now."* Even a compliment wrapped itself in a banal tone of failure.

Surrounded by women, some mechanically minded, some badly made-up, and all envious of one another, the boys had heartily gnawed at their iron bars and unwisely allowed alcohol a free dash at their brains because things overall mattered a little less since their track timings were now a bed of roses and their overall fitness boomed good times ahead, and what harm would a little devilment do? The hair-flicks of the gathered women leant in and leaned forwards and then threw their heads back as they laughed louder than necessary at remarks that weren't especially funny in the first place but that gave opportunity to display expensive and expansive teeth. They clinked and they clanked, darting in and across the hunched revelers as swooping swallows of sensual scents begging for the male mystery to press the female mystery, and knowing with cast-iron assurity that it soon would. Such nights as these cannot ever fail.

Although the publicly confessed lust of the man must always be made to seem ridiculous and prepubescent, the lust of the woman is at first childlike and desperate – as if they know there is something about which they know nothing, and this itch takes on the aggressive – which almost never works. In the bar of cluttered sounds and souls all sorts of things become clear, as if life is about to be launched – or at least lived. Nails parts his legs widely as he slouches back – an open invitation to the women whose eyes dart across in wonder at how the flesh beneath arranges itself (there are such moments, after all, when only basic imagination is required). Women are less of a mystery because their methods and bodies have been over-sold, whereas the male body speaks as the voice calls a halt. The candid and phenomenal superstructure of Tracey is a moving photograph of sex already happening, with her long hesitations and her Elizabeth Taylor non-taming of the shrewd; the alka-seltzer voice, the beer-mat limply twisting erotically over and over in her hands – as if everything must be a prelude to the night's concluding act. The suspense is always held in a performance that must never drop below her usual level, and, in the interests of world sexual enlightenment, it does not. The glare could burn a hole in wood, and touch is transmitted optically. The eyes are there for a reason, and the aim is to use what-ever it is one has, otherwise why have them? Sexual success is a logically given reality, and it simply becomes a question of weighing a sexual force that races ahead of rationale against the great poetry and drama of thought, whilst checking on the time minute-by-minute as if it were ticking towards death (which it is). A new greeter stares firstly into the eyes and then automatically at the mouth, and we all read the entire expanse of each other's faces as we speak. It is never merely a matter of just listening; the face is a page, and the voice might sing as it speaks. Tracey tests Harri teasingly by using her playful instinct of disagreeing with everything that he says so that an explosively defensive passion might burst as eyes of anger at least and at last show resolute intent. Often this backfires, but it is all that she can do, and it is the only way that she can signal to a man that she actually likes him. When he reacts with attack, she knows she has won, for her softening smile will calm crashing currents. In her search for a life that is whole, Tracey would, she freely admits, like a trophy man, and let history judge her otherwise and for other reasons in its due course, but let it also be known that she did, at the very, very least, have her trophy man at some stage. It must be that one man whose name becomes synonymous with her own, and a man whose name alone sums up everything, and whose vomit in the shower would not disgust her. Proust and Chagall were all very well, but it is quite something to release the sex imposed on the mind, and to release it with someone of equal will. Meaningless is the act of kindness from strangers, and hurtful is the sighing one-sided obligation as one watches the clock whilst the other is lost in panic and rush, unable to enjoy the living world now that it finally lands with evangelists' patience. Suddenly a flesh-and-blood figure lies down with you, he of dusky complexion, she free of her very last growing pains whilst knowing each of his eyelashes by heart. This moment shakes the faith of many souls, yet it mostly introduces you to someone you have never before conclusively encountered, and that is: *someone like you who likes someone like you.*

We do not invent it ourselves, and nor do we ask for it, yet it is our job to find the hour when needs might erupt, as salmons defiantly and insanely jump against the tide for … who knows what reason? It is sex that binds us to life, for it is sex that gave us life, and our four athletes are safe nowhere since their imposing physicality says Yes even when saying No. *It's the No that means Yes.* Urgings of want – you feel it if you've hiked this far to this very bar – conclude this day with Tracey and Harri predictably under shared sheets, and with Ezra and Eliza coiled atop discarded throws. Nails and Justy are left behind and go their own way; Nails flopped on the bedroom floor with jaggedly soothing music swirling in the background, and Justy pleasing himself by pleasuring himself in ways that predate religion, and no explanations required. We all do whatever we must. In the bed of Tracey and Harri the physical rush is a floodgate – too fast to mean anything, too many court-jester *ouches* … with their minds already wandering towards whatever will save them in order to make their exit seem polite and timely. In their secrecy, Harri does not like Tracey's knotted banana toes, and Tracey finds the manly central issue too slight to grip, and although such things ought not to count in the adult mind, somehow they do yet they don't yet they do yet they don't.

Mr Rims once grabbed life and then let it go, having no idea that there would be no second chances. *"You'll nail anything that moves,"* they had laughed about him, and from this he felt certain he was alive, catching the biggest fish. Now, coaching allowed him the gaps that he needed in order to slow down and no longer be the principal performer, even though he knew very well that he had aged into a typical case study of a typical type, living suddenly as the shapeless failure whose tired repartee was more than he could adequately explain – to himself, far less than to others. The menace of late middle-age really does, after all,

37

bully its way through, and is not a spoof, and how very little time it took to slip over to the dark side.

He urged the boys to avoid alcohol and excess of physical pleasure, advice that had already aged him, yet which they accepted – largely. Now weary of time, Rims had worn himself out on the very two jewelled pleasures that his finger-wagging drilled through the boys with personal guilt, because, after all, it was for their own good (even if it had not ever been for his). But something for the boys had now changed. A trigger-switch had been clicked and there were too many hot-sweating nightmares of death under shrubbery, and all four had experienced similar dreams of single-track roads with yellow flag irises on either side. Relief would be sought and found. In his own dreams, Rims felt certain he could have very easily forged a manly world in Berlin or Leipzig – wild with passion for women of melancholic eyes and oh so slow, slow movements. Foreign affairs were of no interest to the American military soldier, yet there strode Rims in repaired breeches, loving the male joy of being no different to the rest of the squad marching forth to save the fattened neck of Churchill, whose home country was in an unhealthy and dangerous condition. Thus the U.S. government tore boys from their mother's arms and posted them off to lands empty of experience, where the boys' heads could be split onto spikes. Meanwhile, whilst yelping for help, the British established elite remained cosy and calm in rolling estates behind saxon gates. Churchill himself would experience World War 2 safely and in a suite of rooms at Claridge's most luxurious Mayfair hotel, with not a complicated twitch or pang to trouble his elaborate evening meal, often just he and Ivor

Novello, like dons in senior common rooms, loaded on cognac and crashing into each other with doubled-up laughter, cigar-smoke being as close as they'd ever be to physical danger. Thankfully, the poor will die for us, yet the historic honor will belong only to Churchill, whilst the names of the dead shall never be said, and those who insist upon being known as 'the royals' shall neatly and tartly cocoon themselves away in the preserved luxury of various country seats (as paid for by the dying poor), utilizing any rules within or without the game to avoid getting their hands dirty. This, after all, is what the poor are for, and although the young men of England will die (unasked) to spare the self-elected 'royals' from Nazi Germany, the favor shall never be returned. The welfare of the party above the welfare of the nation is there in the eyes of Churchill, who would be booted out of office as soon as the war ended, so trusted was he at war's end. Although the war against Germany was won, not by Churchill, but by Alan Turing, history would scrub Turing out of existence due to his very private struggle with his own homosexuality, and once the war had been settled (thanks to Turing breaking German secret codes), instead of British authorities lauding Turing as a supernatural agent who unplucked questions too deep for science in a successful effort to save all of England, they instead persecuted Turing's nature towards his convenient act of self-destruction. Nicely out of the way, Turing would only ever be recalled for his suicide, and the UK elite were spared the humiliation of needing to praise a homosexual for saving Britain from Hitler. Instead, all of the praise neatly fell to Churchill, who had at least kept his whispered dalliance with Ivor Novello under Claridge's wraps. 'Queen'

Elizabeth and her mother were also hailed as World War 2 'heroes', having done nothing throughout the war but dine lavishly in protected splendor with their manicured teeth … always … saying nothing, saying nothing, oh so royally saying nothing (lest they say the wrong thing). This is what democracy means. Nothing forever, Rims left his deportments to those who thought they knew better, free to escape to where your freedom is nonetheless still checked. *"Wait for me! And walk in step!"* was a comrade's call made to Rims in Germany, and that soft male voice, and all within it, travelled like the sound of love, and sustained Rims for months to come, even if possibly dying for Churchill and Roosevelt repulsed the Rims of no choice: shoot the enemy or be shot by your own conscripted servicemen … the military wrath shows mercy to none, as all is unfair in love and war. *We Want To Kill YOU!* blared the recruitment posters, as ugly Uncle Sam pointed to those quite certain that they weren't real men unless they were the political cannon-fodder that only death could blue-ribbon.

Now, peace is regained as his television flickers from commercial to commercial to commercial to commercial, advertising nothing at all that he would ever want or need, yet reminding him that *he is* nothing and that he will die in debt, reminding him that whatever insurance he might have could never possibly be enough, reminding him that all medications will kill him mid-laughter, shouting at him as if they were the vigilant society – a blatantly sensational phony inflation with that essential TV ingredient of nightmare and pixy-minded publicity with nothing at all to touch the artistic emotions, yet preying unmercifully on the viewer's insecurity and lack of ready cash. Whatever you can do will never be enough. You are fragile and possibly already dead. Thank God, he thought, for Dick Cavett, who acts through words, who placed questions before viewers in a richly competent way, free of the condescending claptrap trap and always with a direct route to some basic truths. Thank God, he thought, for Dick Cavett, highly civilized enlightenment and peace accomplished – yet there he stood, all-Nebraskan American and costumed in the heart of United States of Generica, yet mysteriously meaningful. *The Dick Cavett Show* reruns transmitted love to Rims nightly, that rare glimpse of television entertainment that dared assume its audience to be in possession of fully formed brain-matter. This, in the United States, was a very rare thing indeed, and possibly treasonable under constitutional laws. Consumption and escape, as the 4 a.m. dreams of Rims would break off into a spinning spindle of whatever he had seen that previous night on *The Dick Cavett Show* – the show that didn't end when it finished. Beer assures Rims that the very best of reality is a friendly pair of eyes and the tender gesture of holding doors open for others, and of excusing intrusion in a small tenderness for women and men that he shall never know. It is now only the little things. Nothing else lives in the heart. He sees teenage girls as he saw them when he too were a teenager, and he cannot bear the fact that they no longer see him – as once they had. A trip to the local mall in search of strip plywood is to look suffering directly in the eyes. Do teenage girls know about men of Rims' age? Well, they know *something*. But they cannot know of the speed of change into an older person, outside of the ring, suddenly a swab-down cornerman instead of a ribbed boxer, suddenly a fat face of bleak monotony swallowed up by life, persecuted by forms and fees and forms and fees and insurance penalties and security threats in the land of the free. Now, as Rims overhears the teen-burst giggle of a gaggle of girls, he automatically frowns, because although he likes the sound, he knows he is hearing the sound of his own grave, for nothing, now, will correct the misshapen bully-boy face that time has given him unrequested. The mentality of our age tells us that men such as he do not exist, or are outside all interesting demographics, for they do not feature on billboards advertising scent or shampoo, yet they might possibly be seen endorsing care homes or fighting a courageous sickness. The expression of transfixed terror is now the only face that Rims has, and he realizes that it will not slip back to the youthful openness of his past countenance of good intentions, because that, simply, is life, and is what life unfailingly does when such as Rims begin to snooze a mid-afternoon nap that revives, yes, but does not repair ravages, as Rims' self-inspection now notes only crumbling, crumbling, crumbling in place of the development of his strengths. Unclothed, the ruin is heartbreaking for Rims ... *and how lucky were they who saw me in glory, standing to attention in more ways than one.*

"How do we find new ways to hand this baton to one another and make it any better than it was?" asks Nails, all kitted and fitted and ready for the new day. *"By being faster, that's all ... by not dropping it ... and by all means kill yourself if needs must ...*

death or gory," answers Justy unhelpfully, looking still young enough to be innocent. The afternoon's jaws yawned. Time moves on as it must, and life becomes a camera-flash of exhilarating fitness regimes, the past a distant nowhere, the future always superior and agreeably laden with unclaimed prizes, praise on all lips, your name printed in local newspapers becoming the sound of moony she-man poetry when read over and over repeatedly, like tolling bells harmonizing their midnight peal; the outcome an inevitable wish fulfilled with nothing at all but jaundiced favoritism to claim and collect … the commemorative ribbon, the constitutional medal, the permissible giddiness, and the self-willed, just achievement having re-written the scriptures. Glory brings its preferential treatments and its smiling partialities. They were the best team in the country, and whether willingly or stubbornly their inevitable success was already recognized in predisposed essays on college forums. Season after season they were known for being known, their timings eagerly canvassed and difficult to become more absolute. This attention brought a certain hateful resentment in proportion to the back-slaps of devotional well-wishers, and the girls of the 'I, unlovely' division who wrote too openly from afar offering unsought personal details with their *this-is-not-me-at-my-best* photographs. The cheerleader is dead, yet is brought to life by the justification to praise and wave and flounce and bounce, and to later break down in private meaninglessness. The tongue, unfortunately, breaks loose on the safety and secrecy of paper whilst suffering in its haste by assuring itself that the sheet shall shield all secrets because, after all, it is only here and now, between you and I, for no one else is reading this. Poisonous dribble is always prepared should a cry go unanswered, and the desire to injure is a critical shade of the fiery enthusiast, for since no one can love you as much as I do, therefore no one can likewise exceed my venom. Accept the enslavement of my undying love, or bear my viciously unpleasant cruelty, for dearly I love you more than any other could.

Shadowed against bored sunlight our boys despaired to ever again recall the wasted heap whom none had yet reported as a thrillingly grisly find, so woven into stretching vegetation, ripped in the jaws of ravenous rats and grunting boars and stalking hawks. Human flesh when devoured is said to differ not at all from the flesh of pigs. Owls would sniff the stiff and make off with frosted eyeballs as the fox family unglue and rip at this medley of meatball. In the church of secret service known as the abattoir this is exactly what humans excitedly do to beautiful bodies of animals who were also crafted in care by some divine creationist, yet at the human hand the animals are whacked and hacked into chopped meat whilst gazing up at their protector with disbelief and pleading for a mercy not familiar to the human spirit, ground and round into hash or stew for the Big Mac pleasure of fat-podge children whose candidature for roly-poly vicious porkiness makes their plungingly plump parents laugh loudly, as little junior blubber-guts orders yet another Superburger with tub-of-guts determination to stuff death into round bellies, and such kids come to resemble their parents as ten pounds of shit in a five-pound bag.

Knees pumped a canine scamper as yet another Tuesday had Ezra hotfoot ahead, passing on that in-the-saddle baton to Nails, who pedaled with both feet to an out-stretched Harri. *"Sko!"* called Justy, *"Sko! Sko! Sko!"* his economic version of *"Let's go!"*, and the stumps stirred further and further. Commentary in college newsletters repeatedly warned of this very locomotion machine whose bolt had been logged and filmed and photographed for every enviable stubby pumpkin in every corpulent Pepsicola tank town from South Succotash to the boondock boonies beyond so that they might rightfully shrink with unmerry-go-round doubt at the mighty Priorswood. Soon shall be the finish of that final competing moment when landsmen and compadre were no more; their killer instincts killed, their do-or-die done. Mumblings of a new dark-horse shadow ghost from Philadelphia raised a tribal alarm squawk here and there, but rarely here and infrequently there since there wasn't sufficient soul to statistically pitch battle against the tight mob-ring of campesino Priorswood. The anger of straggling teams pitched their bitchery and cried into their rolled towels, but only Ezra's famiglia had the unfortunate tiger by the unfortunate tail, and any hurt vanity would not be Ezra's. Scoreboard summaries listed student stats fairly – and with stethoscope intimacy as medical charts were watched with nitpicker's fussiness lest whispers of 'roid rage (the excitable mania produced by pancake layers of steroids) sleazed up the reputation of any team peppy enough to sniff victory in advance.

Away from the track Ezra and Eliza were, by now, com-patible enough to ignore the very worst of each other's habits. Their names were now so tightly super-glued that toastmasters began to joke with some seriousness about marital union (*"please make the same mistake that we did, so that we shan't feel so patsy-pigeoned"*) – so frothy and pawed and finely tuned were the doves. By now, Ezra would head up the mountain at will, whilst Eliza was always quite happy with bed and breakfast. Eliza was a fierce grabber, which was another first for Ezra, who had only known gentle intention. Eliza barged in intemperately, kicking up heels and kicking up a racket, and even here, now, Ezra secured a particular teamwork – all meat and potatoes, nuts and bolts. Eliza drove with no brakes, as if supplies were dwindling, as if the seven-year-old within couldn't quite believe what it was that lay beside her, or how much happiness she brought to his eyes by doing what she thought to be nothing at all. The locked position when Ezra rubbed as far as he could go; the hump and bump of injection as his eyes met hers in equal swirl – guts and innards finally melting with intellect as jets of Ezra would cut in and then cut off at that moment when all of the body is felt from tip to toe; the inside works just as well as the outside. With playful nastiness, Eliza twists her entire body as she pulls away, knowing that this will cause neatly burning pain to Ezra – which amuses her because it brings to Ezra's face a new expression, like inhaling a cigarette, that face … that landscape … how could he see his own reflection every single day and not feel blessed? Eliza's sudden twist is an awakening hurt unlike their earlier tit-for-tat punch-ups, after which Ezra falls flatly on his front – pinned on the rack like a sailor receiving the lash with a wordless intoxication as a light wave of the hand gives Eliza the all-passions-spent tip-off. She could, of course, make further demands, but enough has taken place. The mutual head-rush struck both of them at the same time, as a man-and-woman lightning bolt that meant they could now lounge together at the end of it, yet saying nothing, because the air around their silence crashed and gargled with so much meaning. The sight of her discarded shoes by the end of the bed caused the fire in his belly to burn up; yes, just something that simple, a frenzied symbol of all cylinders burning, and all clocks ticking in his favour. Likewise, as he walked away from the bed, Eliza would examine the braced-up rhythm of Ezra's muscled back, arms and legs, as the entire V man assaulted all of her sensibilities, for here it now was – nailed down and won, as love takes its unquestioned and dignified place, and long years of spiral-notebook alone-ness are suddenly difficult to recall as the bewail of virginity now seemed like harmless comedy – but only because it had ceased, replaced by such knowing airs.

Certain that he was alone in the house, Harri wearily lumbered down the stairs wearing only his white briefs as he squinted from the dazzle of an overdone 9 a.m. sun that cut through the house wherever it could. By now his mother would have left for her Tuesday morning custodial charity stint at a local hostel, where best wishes and the squarest of meals would always do for those in embarrass-ing circumstances. Mother was a forgotten saint of indestructibly strong core, ready for any sudden stirring to help the hopeless, psychologizing over vats of spaghetti and the donated suits of the war dead, monastically freez-ing concentrated facial expressions as she endured pointless chats with the socially disconnected whose lives had all but exhausted them out of existence. We hear so often of smiling prosperity and plentiful gains, yet it is thought unwise to mention the other America, even though the truth of it all crouches disjointedly in the hidden America and not at all in the inherently unstable pious vision of plenty. Harri's mother was drawn to those who carried their small lives in small bags, for everyone was there to be saved, no matter how diminished their will. On this very morning, Harri floated into the kitchen, where what at first seemed like assembled rags lay muddled and messy beneath the kitchen table. *What on earth was mother collecting now?* A terrible darkness of great depth and sweep executed Harri's body as what lay ruffled before him registered. He softly placed his right palm across his mother's head – she now so cold and absented. A secret of nature spoke, and he knew, and he gently knelt before the unreturning. Instantly he was no longer as he had ever been, for the voice of love had gone – fired away to the inescapable suffering. Still kneeling, Harri travelled speedily through time – his time, his mother's time, and as he looked at love he saw the cruelty that must always make the final claim, and he looked into the oblivion that no one gives any heed to until it wins their final breath. Immobilized by physical pain, Harri's body shivered and shuddered as the minutes passed like hours; see the hands he knew as well as his own, see the first he knew of touch and sound, and the soothing patterns of her carefully chosen clothes. *Immortal, indestructible mother is dead.* This moment is too delicate to infringe upon, to pass over to know-all medics who examine insurance policies more thoroughly than they examine the recumbent victim … in the land of the brave and the home of the free. Too fragile a moment to rush through and blot over with police reports and a chapter-and-verse blow-by-blow of what's what and where it's at, the size of it and the straight of it all jotted down so desultorily and indifferently by the kitchen police. This moment is far too strong to articulate, being beyond the capacity of feeling and language, and no no no no no, it is not happening, it is not happening, and mother dear, I cannot put your beloved body into the hands of bossy interference. Though gone from daylight, she whose happiness had always been his happiness, here was still their last moment together.

Winter atmosphere now fogged its way through the house, for the house had held mother's soul and was now inhospitable without that soul, falling back into darkness as if infected by rage at the loss of its keeper. Now, the house was nothing at all, frozen by helium blast. The secret heart asked mother one final question: how do I now get close to you? But the question is too pitiful or just too late. Ah, but mother dear, I shall be the prop of your old age, and let it fall squarely on my shoulders for there is far too much for you to feel responsible for ... as units of time become units of distance and mother mutates into memory, and oh, so many questions I had wanted to ask you, and oh, so many new things that I can't wait to tell you ... but cannot. Sunny-natured, I shall take your arm, and together we shall always punch aside hastening death. There would always be time, and death has already taken so many others that it cannot possibly need you. There would always be time. But now Harri felt a pain that others could only guess at, and here was the very first day of his life that would not pass as all other days had. Here was his first moment of aloneness, no longer someone's son, no longer someone's baby, and although a new wisdom shook his brain it was a wisdom that he had no wish for, as horror itself went insane. Gazing into hell he saw the thin line between suffering and mental deficiency, and only darkness could be a relief from such unimaginable rapids of fastidious torment. Unversed in practicalities, Harri very slowly telephoned the elderly lady who lived next door, and he explained the inexplicable to Margo in a voice sounding nothing like his own, and somehow not believing the words being skewered out of his own mouth. Margo knew that people are allowed to be dead, and she had seen many a sudden and surprise ending. Calmly, and with that independent technique of a world long gone, Margo assured Harri that she could call all necessary signals and take control, and her eighty-four years rolled into motion like a rocket-fueled missile, fully resourceful on a day when life rotted. *"It's very hard to accept that your powers are limited,"* she later explained to Harri, and the sun struck at a certain angle like a hint from nature that there would certainly be another tomorrow, and that it ought to be lived.

Harri declined to attend his mother's funeral because he felt that he had already done so during the hours that he sat on the kitchen floor with her dry, organic remains, with all of its requirements and grasping insistence of control over conflict, control of explosion … the body against the soul … the limited against the boundless. He wanted people to know how much he was suffering at the loss of his mother, yet his shaky duty was to hide it from them.

"There was only she and I," he softly explained to Ezra at Ledger's Bar, the voice consistently croaking a half-crack, *"and the life she led was the life I led. What makes tomorrow worth anything?"*

"*Me!*" shouted Ezra. "*Everything we've worked for these last eighteen months! She would want you winning … not sick with grief. I loved your mother, too. But we need you …*" His voice trailed away unconvincingly, knowing that Harri was neither listening nor captive. The week worsened as weakly Harri sat alone at Ledger's Bar. He is now slipping away, yet he has adjusted to the sensation of feeling worn, for there is not a single kind thought within him and he could accommodate no more of the inherently decent advice that spun his way from caring friends. Margo had been genuinely good, caring and accommodating without self-interest. Even though Harri didn't actually know her very well, she had discreetly assisted as much as she could with the house, offering soothing aromas of wood crackling warmth and confidence and cooking that might renew Harri moment by moment, preventing him from sliding into further dramatic shock. Margo attempted to spruce and brighten the big icy blackness of the now deadly sealed rooms. Small touches here and there worked miracles: the warming smells of home cooking, quietly soothing classical radio, decency and empathy from the frame of this small woman who quietly replicated mother's habits of lighted candles and neat bedding and laundered towels spelling out peace preserved and motivated only by love. As noble as Margo's efforts were, she didn't know Harri well enough to become a powerful authority in his life, and, although genial to the last, she could only manage some light housework. Margo had seen a body die and then had witnessed a spirit die, and the former was easier to deal with. Gallantly, she would fall asleep on a downstairs recliner so that Harri might sleep an untroubled sleep assured that the heart of a civilizing influence occupied the room below, and that he was not quite so adrift.

Another night passed at Ledger's Bar as a small, ageless figure ripe from the underground spoke cautiously to Harri. *"I've got what you want,"* it said.

"You … what?" asked Harri, looking down from his barstool.

"Horse, snow, white sugar, brown sugar, aitch, Mexican mud, Chinese red … black Russian, blond Lebanese …" The little mud puppy squirreled on.

There came a thoughtful pause as Harri examined this running dog, a twirl of a scag-trade pharmacy. *"But do you have enough?"* asked Harri, somehow done with it all. The toad of hell smiled a persuader's smile as the rag-mop transaction took place, during which Harri caught a shadowed sight of the man's face in the awkwardly dull lighting of Ledger's Bar. Dummied and tight-lipped, the face was empty of meaning, yet the savage granite expression aroused a certain tension. What was it? The inscrutable glacial coldness of the mega-gnarly cave-dweller had brought to mind the snot-nosed wretch that the boys had left to the woods. But this could only be irrelevant coincidence – or, to the esoteric world, not coincidence at all. As if it were his life's worth, Harri took care not to slip on the stairs as he climbed for the final time towards his childhood bedroom, a friendly room of trophies and teenboy artifacts that foolishly become souvenirs of scuzzed-up years. Harri slumped to the floor heavy-headed and heavy-hearted, striving to conclude the day with a certain patience and wisdom. He shall travel this path without the strength to cope with anything else, no longer likely to explode from this intensity, yet ready to fuse the physical with the spiritual and to accept that the next moment will be unlike any other. Life had become much too burdensome, and the repulsive vision of his mother's cashed-in body and soul all alone under soil caused a brittle left-to-right cluster headache each time its flash-photography image tasered his brain. Here was a point of control whereby you are your own witness, and all that happens is made by you and does not need further clarification. Let the minutes spin as a tankard of vodka is clouded by a heavy overjolt of brown and white powder, both of which submerge like falling snow as they enjoy one another and whisper, *I'm the right friend for you.* Harri lies back in order to wait – on this very bed, bought so early in his teens, of nights that brought him a little of everything that over-active fantasy and imagination could possibly muster, and that were now only important as quaint flickers of flashing recall. *Were you ever really that small, that trusting … that raucous tweenager? So loud! So loud! A flight of stairs with two leaps!* Now, each fast gulp of the cloudy cocktail spared nothing, and three fierce swigs empties the tankard with an earth-rattling speed – even now, allowing contemplation no access. A sleepiness demanded further sleep. *"I lived – here's proof,"* he said, smiling as he raised a boyhood pewter trophy before him to lovingly inspect, yet now realizing that he could no longer control the body that had earned it. In endless fidget he had shed all responsibility without losing trust in his own intuition, and for once he had no right to expect his body to behave well, for … why should it? There came a nobility to his expression as his head sunk further back into the built-up pillows, yet a loud and unpleasant ringing had begun in both ears. There was no way to get out of it now. The pulp of his hands were the pals of the dying, and suddenly his face was wet as his lower abdomen felt the punch of a fierce doubled-up bolt and a grinding, knotted twist. He was aware of the pain but also of its completeness and necessity. It was at once inhospitable yet he felt immune to enemy fire, because the now-rising screech in his head humanized him as his eyes closed like a book and he accepted that he was now behind it or beyond it and there was no need to think further on the matter and he was a child again on a bed of cast iron and there were waiting rooms of doctors and an elderly lady in black who was neatly dressed as she leaned over his bed and asked *"Are you ready now? Are you ready to go now?"* and he saw himself unborn and he whispered *"Yes, thank you,"* with an infant's sigh, and there were no longer uncertainties about whatever was right or wrong as his eyes began to swell and something stronger than himself took charge, arranging him to a nothingness of abnormal heart rhythms and voluntary unconsciousness in which the mind's eye saw a Sunday in a simplified life, always restless and full of fun, yet this woman in volcanic black returned unexpectedly with *"Are you ready now?"* and he remembered that he had already told her that he was, and the taste of the blood in his mouth only made him smile for he knew there would be no bouncing back like late-night waves unseen from the beach yet sounding as if all around, because, as the brain began to vomit, he was quickly beginning to die.

Locked together in a triangular scrum embrace of strong arms and choked sobs, our heroes Ezra, Nails and Justy stood a few yards away from the gathered mourners of heads bowed, staring in shock at the lowered coffin as if imagining their inevitable turn within; we cry for ourselves when we cry for others. As the priest gibbered and jabbered his dutiful dribble, from the roadside came the blaring disco music of a passing open-topped car, and the skimble-skamble of senseless children from the funeral crowd suddenly broke loose and began to screech excitedly and run in circles. All at once nothing at all made sense. Even the clouds lowered unexpectedly, and the cluster of the knowingly nodding sympathetics moved stiffly, as if on their very best behavior, none knowing what to say in order to avoid even one misplaced word, all tripping gently as they moved away from the grave. It is a wordless day, in fact, for there are none to adequately sum it all up, for how could there be? The priest prattled confidently whilst reading a book of debatable origins, and the mourners mourned in the way that mourners must mourn in fear of not seeming to genuinely mourn. Margo candidly cried running tears for all – of past, present and future.

"He isn't in that box, is he?" sobbed Justy; *"how could he be?"* he trailed away.

"Ledger's?" came Ezra's brave suggestion, and he pointed to the cemetery gates in the southerly corner of the plot.

"First in no pay?" Nails felt rejuvenated, and with a ferocious tear they pushed each other away from their fierce embrace and they bolted manically through, over and across; around all of the variously sized stones and monuments that blocked their dash to the southerly gates; hurdle after hurdle, legs wide and sprawled and full of kangaroo sideways swerves through the Jewish section, whilst galloping even faster across the Polish Garden and

laughing all the while as faster and faster went the trio, from gallop to glide, their neatly solemn suits askew and awry with messy devilment; Ezra nosing ahead, Justy of yelps and fearful moans as each stone tablet varied in jutting awkwardness, with some to maneuver around and some to breeze above … *"Yeeeey!"* came Nails with high-flying gusto … dodging the Sacred Heart, leap-frogging St. Francis, crashing down onto unvisited graves of unwedded maidens, kicking up soil and the tish-tosh knick-knacks of *Gone but not forgotten, always in our hearts, just a whisper away, Loving Brother, taken too soon, World's Best Grandma, reunited in heaven, Our Little Angel* … uncle unmarried unwanted and gone, the stampede paid no heed to respectful consideration as depleted bouquets flicked wildly under kicks, and our three became lost tearaway children turning anger into Benylin adrenalin … through the gates and through main-street traffic lanes, woo-hooing their illegalities and delighted stupidities of funeral fun … *why always remain in control?* Who's to say what should or should not lift the spirits? Whoever put the pain in painting had also put the fun in funeral. But why always stand there, zombified, awaiting life's WALK sign? Are you now incapable of walking unless instructed? *Harrieee … Harrieee …* Harri underground whilst we remain above, and here is an afternoon to waste as we'd wish! And soaked we shall be at Ledger's, where ties are removed like shackles of subjugation and the bottles line up and the whiskey doesn't touch the sides as it sinks as today's thinking man's drink.

Later that night our trio lie on college towels sprawled across tiled floor as gentle jets of water spray like Japanese rain on the huddled far-gone three in the otherwise deserted after-hours sigh of the college locker rooms; bombed and smashed they lay on their backs, their skunk-drunk faces rising upwards and into the falling spray, a long necklace of wartime bombs shelling the children of the sleeping city. Shut up hearts sprang open as the wide and steamy jet-stream managed to bounce off all three faces as they lay back, shoulder to shoulder, boulder to boulder, their clothes abandoned in single-file brotherhood trail from doorway to shower-head. *"I wouldn't change me for the woooorld,"* started Nails in a singsong outcry … *"**Who** disturbs my peace?"* clamors Justy … *"Me does!"* splits Nails' throat … *"You must be suck-out-loud buzzed … and I mean that in the most caring way of course,"* is a waul of a squall from Ezra … *"Youze cookin' with gas!"* yelps yappy Nails … *"God will repay me as he always does …"* carries on Ezra … *"Well, he doesn't repay me … still driving that El Camino"* … *"You just said you wouldn't change you for the world,"* blurts Ezra, and the silliness goes on. *"I'd kiss my own little face if I could. This thankful bodily creation lying next to you,* mi amigo, *truth in my heart, no legs stronger or finer, it's all in my favor and stirring with manhood … or somethinghood."* Nails cannot be stopped.

"But where is Harri now? In repose, repose, repose? In turmoil? In nothing? Human roadkill? In nothingness? Why were we not reason enough for him to stay? Are we really so bad?" Justy offers the sweet and the sour.

"I'd say … yes," pipes in Nails, *"death a dark falling … someone said … Harri just so … one last heave, journey to go."*

"Let me press that to my heart!"

"Weep yourself clean, my man!"

"Great sweeping thoughts I can barely grasp … just all day …

I see his face in his final hour ... and where was I when he needed someone? I was matter-of-fact, somewhere else, and useless ..."

"You mustn't keep asking yourself how you're feeling. There isn't a lesson to be learned from every single thing you do!"

"Then why do them? Why do anything?"

"And if I should stop asking myself how I feel then I shan't apply this lesson, because if I apply what you've just said then I'm asking how —"

*"Oooh **shut up**, tool you ..."*

"Oh sweet mother, tool you? That's tough."

"I have a small head. It can't contain much. It will grow on you as it grew on me."

"Now. Your leg is touching my leg, which is all very nice, but I think of you more as a friend."

"Ah yes! Sorry! God forbid a leg touches another leg and the entire foundation of rigid sexual mores crash to shuddering, shamed failure!"

"He'd walk across the field ... towards me ... with that strong stride and stupid with smiles, and I'd be happy just to hear whatever the hell would stream out of him on that day, on any day ... that open face, that knowing grin ... that grin I'd known all of my life ... before we'd even met. I grew up on tales of his exploits, I knew his body like I knew my own."

At this stage it hardly mattered who was saying what, since all were in a whiskey-soaked lecturer's tub-thumping tirade.

"Everything's a question! Everything's a question! Isn't it?"

"I press that to my heart," said Ezra.

"Weep yourself clean!" shouts Nails.

"I'd drink poison for our man!"

"Well, let's see if you'll drink poison for this one," cut in the un-expected monotone of Mr Rims, suddenly appearing in the locker-room with a champion-styled candidate. *" He'll behead, blow up, strangle ... whatever you need to get that June cup."*

"Yes, but can he run?" wised-in Nails.

"Don't try to be witty, it doesn't suit you and it doesn't work and it's upsetting. I give you ... Dibbs, and you'll take Dibbs because you want him and you need him, and that's that, so shut up."

Like a ghost ungone, the shell-backed Rims had appeared unexpectedly as if getting his own back in his search for the last word. As a reluctant pallbearer, he had noticed earlier the three Boston tearabouts flee the scene of sobs and dart like buffos of a new age across to the southerly gates leading to nowhere logical other than Ledger's. From here, Rims underwent the bone-splitting agony of deserting Dick Cavett slowness in order to track the tracksters down with trap-tackle and force them face-to-face with the dog on a chain known as Dibbs. Dead and reborn numerous times, the boys now listened to Rims as life moved until whatever is meant to happen next happens next. Arranged like cut flowers, Dibbs was good at pulling faces whilst looking like nothing worth taking seriously (but what were the rest if not saddened and searching youth?). A non-verbal entity, Dibbs struggled with all of the certainty of someone who obviously knew too little, and with a language unknown, slopped into a mess of one who blathers for the sake of blathering. Look at these knotholes posing as sprinters (or is the appalling word 'spinsters'?) and welcome, welcome to a new walled paradise. Our three rise and offer gentlemanly handshakes – friendly nods and murmurs of welcome. Dibbs beamed as fresh young life of wide smiles and bending-over-backwards confidence – a power hitter of herky-jerky motions. The boys drank him in as Dibbs laughed a deep and warm laugh whenever anything was said, be it amusing or not. *"I run for beer!"* he announced, desperate to crack into mounds of unbreakable ice, desperate to replace the irreplaceable.

Mr Rims was soapbox ready: *"A virtuous emblem remains to be left on the age, and here is the man to save our spirits and eat fire, as we learn as professional athletes that we must take the bad days in the same spirit as the good. Half of your life has not been worth living if you let this opportunity go. Harri has slipped from us, and we're all just a few yards away from the emotional edge, but I tell you that a light shines at the far end – the far end now being closer than it once was, of course – and it is acceptable to stand upright and to resume because it all remains to be done and you'll evoke only eternal pity if you miss this particular bus."* At this stage, everyone had stopped listening to Mr Rims, but he continued regardless. *"You already possess all that you need, and with Dibbs here you'll find every answer in a return to the track. The track to where, you wonder? What's at the end of that track? Well, pride and joy shall be there, and Harri would want you to continue at his urging, and if you don't believe me then just suffer. I don't want to feel that I'm running up against a brick wall just by pointing these damned things out. I could be at home pulverizing my wife at Scrabble, or scrabbling my pulverized wife, so don't think I don't have far more sophisticated things to do. Winning will tell the truth about all of you because you've worked hard for it and you've earned it and proof of everything is in your cannonball conduct, and, yes, inner resolve is one thing, but the outer reality counts just as much, and it's not as if you have anything else to contribute to earthly wisdom. There is indeed a God who helps athletes win against opponents. Harri is gone, and you must accept that and go beyond it because the alternatives help neither yourselves nor those unfortunates around you. We are all fully dependent on unforeseen circumstances. Do your best to prove to yourself that the pain does not exist. Don't be saddened by having felt Harri's loss, but instead take a broader view and feel all the richer for having known him. He's not gone anywhere that we aren't heading ourselves. There's nothing unique about his journey. Let the public see what they've invested in you for so long now, and Dibbs here – for all the silliness of his name – is not so easily intimidated on the track. I can't speak for elsewhere, and I have no interest. Now, with relief I ask you to dry off and get dressed and then get to know this speed demon and I know he'll restore your faith and ambition and you will be on track at 8 a.m. tomorrow eager to maintain your true selves and your reputation like no other spring and sprint college team known in this competition. Feelings must carry into deeds, otherwise what's the point of those feelings in the first place … we don't have feelings in order to do nothing with them. Sleep in your own beds tonight and I do assure you that you'll awake with an increased level of pride knowing how Dibbs – for all the silliness of his name – has all your assets and asses covered … an area growing considerably in recent weeks, it must be noted. Now get your pretty little village faces out of here and take full heed of what passes between us. I'm neither cold nor indifferent to Harri's death, but nothing you or I can do will bring him back, and the only way to deal with it is to accept it. But we don't crack under duress. What you can give you will still give under my watch, and the world will applaud and delight in your open-throttle vocation. Do I make myself clear? Or is my expression not quite intense enough? I'd prefer to stop talking whilst I'm still clean-shaven."*

Mists of pain shifted and all four boys smiled broadly. Newness began again. Preliminary chatter rose with a stark-tiled echo, and then out into darkness they slackly dragged their sports bags and track tackle amid excited whispers of possibilities. Ezra gestured an *I'll catch up with you* wave as he dawdled slightly in the barren barracks-styled washroom where necessity raced him into one of the bathroom stalls where, once seated, he rolled out a college events calendar in order to relax his mind enough to allow grand expulsion. The faint drip of a shower-nozzle, very distant slamming of car doors, but there was none of the echo-chamber clatter of epic daytime shrieks and goading gabble that fill these rooms during studious hours. Now, with midnight minutes away, Ezra sat in the eerie silence of a college with no afterlife when unoccupied, and it dies a fast execution without its busy and odorous humans, as a subterranean hush washes through the halls and the building simply cannot live. At nighttime the rooms are spirited away, unable to manage convincing sleep, unable to be anything at all minus its sludgeball students, as life leaves its old soul – as if these bricks and glass thrive only on human blood, and graveyard corridors sob softly with the despair at having no use once the pock-faced pygmies have gone to their homes to moan. The building remains as the stroppy scholars had left it, and it waits for resuscitation when revived by the return of the algebraic washed and the naked life of the brain-dead well-fed. As Ezra sat scrutinizing the sports pages of honor-mad rah-rah teams … *Man of the Month, One to Watch, the latest league charts* … he felt an arm gently resting around his own right arm, making the same cradling shape as Ezra's own and pressing in warmly as if to shake awake. Ezra stared intently at his arm and then he jumped in sprite fright to lean his full body against the left-side wall of the stall, pulling away from this mysterious sensation. Powerful orbit jetted Ezra out of the 'johnny house' and into the large washroom, where he scrambled to organize his clothes and pull himself together as a rush of unholy phobia and stampeding blind panic told him instinctively that he was in a place that he ought not to be – and in a moment that one ought not to play about with. Timorously a voice then spoke to him with a gentle apprehension, of suffering and terror, of disheartening qualm, so terrified in itself that Ezra felt immediate calm at the sight of the small elfish woman standing pressed into the corner of the room. The human frailty held onto the wall for support, a shrunken and concave visualization that looked as if released from her own grave, in desperately poor health, of distressed hair, and inexplicably cloaked in layers of interwoven garments. Her voice posed no threat to Ezra other than the shock of actually hearing it, and he concealed his fear as his eyes burned into the enslaved creature before him. She spoke with humble yet powerful insistence, torn with a sick desire.

"*Make an exception …*" she began, "*in my case … and listen to me as an act of kindness, I beg of you. I offer you no harm and I am incapable of such. There is none to whom I can turn. I suffer greatly in painful silence and I speak to you, now, with servitude whilst also pleading for your understanding. I am alone and I agonize in an exasperated state. Is it within your heart to help me be at rest with the one and only thing I have ever loved?"*

"What-is-it?" stuttered Ezra, his voice a half-shout. She moved a few inches closer, without removing her outstretched arm from the wall that balanced her, and Ezra now caught the full shape of her face, so frozen in dejection and want.

"Justifications are unnecessary. I am forever trying my best to speak up, so forgive me should I falter, but here it is. To the rear of the long-disused Gate Lodge on the grounds of this very property there is a heavily shaded area where stretches of sackcloth and tarred tarpaulin have for twenty full years covered out-moded garden equipment of hoe and plow and wheelbarrow and lawnmower and hedge-trimmer gadgets and bicycles that none shall ride again ... all neatly blanketed by a durable covering of weather-soaked layers of sheet metal, now pinned into the ground from years of rainfall and fastening wind, undisturbed for all of twenty longer than usual years. Unseen from the road, and forgotten by all who work at this college, there is no reason for anyone to stray towards this forsaken nook with oak trees weeping down upon it and boxing it in. Beneath the mess of meshed filth and cluttered litter lies a human child, well, no longer human to others perhaps, once buried like a rabid dog, for his life could offer no continual purpose to his resolute murderer. The boy was my son, molested and butchered by a man who had enticed with such kindness, one I am able to name, now, as the very dean of this college – you know him well, whose advancing age is a problem and whose kindly kindred soul belies what lies beneath the forgiving and indulgent shell, for none could believe him capable of the cruelty he bestowed on my own child, now wrapped in vigorous sheets of cold plastic beneath rusted machinery, so deeply unjust and murdered by power maniacs ruled and owned by the sick desires of career and money,

such honorable local citizens of position with their almost satanic over-valuation of a family life that they secretly despise, their coded references to my sweet boy – a boy who had nothing and knew nothing and did no one harm, and for this he was sodomized with hatred and bloodlust and bigotry … And they, and their all-powerful benevolent God, allowed my boy not another day to live. Dean Isaac might now appear timorous, but this is no reason to forgive how he behaved when he was strong."

"What is it you want me to do?" asked Ezra in a wavering whisper, his clothes still undone, his eyes wide with some doubts that whatever it was that was happening was actually happening at all.

"Elizabeth Barbelo is my name, and my son was Noah. Before another day rushes in would you, as an act of humanity, rescue what remains of my boy and bless him with the dignity of a just burial? Only then could I find some ease. I would begin my rest, my trial ended, and the horror of these twenty years I would take as acceptable. I was nobody at all throughout my entire life … and I am recalled by no one, even now … but only the living can end my pain and release me from this terrible dark force, each day a renewed terror."

"I will do as you ask," said Ezra, and the woman's head fell at the weight of her tears, sobs which developed into hacking and cracking coughs as the severe and agonized face looked away with an embarrassment both shy and humble.

"In pitiless solitude I give you what thanks I can … if you would please forgive my overstated gratitude. Marooned as I am in the events of these last twenty years of tears, you will allow me to close out the dreadful past and you will allow me to rest every aching bone, to seal my son's life from womb to tomb with a dignified distinction afforded to even the most cruel and evil of beings, yet denied my dear and loving

son. Your actions will forever live in my heart, as you will forever be nearest the heart. I take my first hour of slumber, for you have removed the knife from my back. Without your help my despair would see no chance of hope. I would wish upon no mother this darkest of dark shadows. I humble myself to nothing before you, for it is agonizing for a mother to have full responsibility for an outcome over which she has no control. I have sought compassionate listeners for many years. You must please forgive my unrestrained sentiment. My only prayer is that he may lie beneath a stone bearing his name … Was he not worth that, at least, instead of the evil and derelict design that befell him – discarded as worthless waste? My life with my son was modest and resigned, lowly and marked by struggle, yet savored minute by minute for our deep feelings of love and for our combined laughter, our friendship, and for that joy of natural affection … You see, he is me."

She made the sign of the cross with an outstretched hand and in the monotheist's way of cupping the index finger from mouth to chest to left then right shoulder, throwing the gesture Ezra's way. She turned too quickly and swept out of the room as if on castors. In the hallway Ezra knew that there would be no sight of her even though any earthly creature would have still been visible … shrinking towards a shadowy beyond-the-stars exit.

"I can't forget that battered, motherly face," cried Ezra as he sat hunched and downcast at the kitchen table. There were tears in the eyes of the boy who wouldn't cry. Around him, Eliza, Nails and Justy took up different parts of the kitchen, either standing or sitting or sloping, with their hands

clasping their faces in stooping and bending despair as they listened to the full account. None would dare breathe as they sank into the deflation of Elizabeth Barbelo's visitation, and to the cruelty meted out to her son. Where, they wondered, was God? *Any God?* If Satan could be capable of so many assignations, then why wasn't God also at hand? If God had been the God of so many miracles, then why had he ceased his mission of miracles? Why halt?

"How are we meant to act on this when you can barely believe it yourself?" asked Eliza, half whine, half demonstration.

"I haven't asked you to act on anything! Every ache of this woman cried out for release … and I … will not … let her down," Ezra now had the look of madness, *"for even to contest her words would be wrong. I have the power and the means to return her child to her … wait … what am I saying?"*

"But where is she now and was she even real?" shouted Eliza, mid-panic.

"Her dread was real. I can't guarantee what she was or where she came from or where she went to, and I'd be rightfully strapped to an iron bed if I began to warn people of haunted locker rooms. I've taken in too much, and I've revealed more honesty to you tonight than anyone else would feel comfortable with."

All three instinctively enveloped Ezra with a wrap of tender loving arms.

"It's almost one o'clock," began Ezra, a slight rocking to his body, whether of power or anger, yet also a fortification as he attempted to shake off his sadness. *"We have access to the college grounds if we approach by the old coast road, and there are shovels and spades, trowels, forks in the garage, and please don't think I'll ever sleep until I at least take this woman's words to mean what they say."*

"Is that you down there, Ezra?" came the voice of Ezra's father, unseen at the top of the stairs.

"Noooooooooooo!" called back Ezra.

"Oh, good," said his father, returning contentedly to bed.

A golf bag hid the digging equipment as the four shifted quietly into the college grounds and across to the sordid spot, shaded by a shambles of overhanging oak trees – indistinct in its permanent protective darkness. Here, the vigilantes pulled at stubborn shrubbery of bramble, brier, scrub and brush; the gnarl of knotted tree-roots and trunk of bough and branch. Thickset greenery twisted into sprigs of twigs and underbrush of stem and stalk. Heavy out-house doors were lacquered with sprouting germination and curly grass, and climbing fern wrapped possessively around perished bicycles. Woodworm waste scattered along with reptile-like millipedes that raced across tick and larva and maggot. Earthworms wiggled annoyance at the disturbance, and termites chased for cover as spade and shovel sliced into gnat and midge territory. Magnetic force had the boys tugging and pulling and lifting with anticip-ation of dread fused with victory-lap excitement. Eliza cautiously supervised surveillance as Priorswood slept a deep valium sleep of fatted contentment, and security lights within the grounds were few and not directed towards the excavation spot where the now-disturbed earth sank and stank messily into a sloppy plop ditch that was likely and willing to swallow up any defeated posture. Ezra, Nails and Justy swung ferociously with spade to soil, heatedly seeking a verdict, deeper into the ground of soggy bog where sunlight could neither reach nor imagine, and thus the marshy mire wallowed a swampy wetness of peat bog, when suddenly a sound like the crust of dry land. *Something.* Arrogant assurance pushed a soaked Ezra, and Nails slipped further into the clammy clay with an even stronger impulse as the minutes ticked like seconds. Their feet and legs now covered in quicksilver slime, their demand began to push even more forcefully, punishing them as the gulch slipped into a gorge of filth now five feet in depth, as Justy's feverishly scraping trowel slid across a stretch of tarpaulin. The ice was broken, and they knew, and they knew, and they knew, and then there came a sight that further darkened the sky. They froze with a shivering fixity, making no moves, saying nothing, paralyzed by what the immediate minutes would reveal and how this would re-position their lives, and how, and what, and if, and when. Without thinking, they simply knew, at that moment when details become evidence immune to debate or argument.

"By unearthing this body we also unearth the murderer. You realize this?" said Eliza, uncharacteristically shaking.

"Yes!" thundered Ezra, firing his spade further into the ground, *"and don't make the mistake that such bloodthirsty evil is human and worthy of any consideration ... don't, don't, don't!"*

Spades wading into despair, they were instantly repaid for their stubborn obstinacy. The outline of a small skeletal frame choked its way through the mud and unfolded from its straitjacket of humiliation as a shrunken but human-shaped figure of life and death, now slain remains in earthen clay, floating through the tarpaulin ... condemned to extinction simply for ... being there at the appointed hour, and he had been waiting for you at your mercy for twenty silent years. In stillness, the clump was

69

unidentifiable, yet what it had been was obvious, and the mouth open widely in silent shout indicated the grisliness and brutality of its final minutes. All four witnesses cried softly, muttering invectives, their arms now wrapped about each other as they looked down upon the most distressing sight of their lives, asphyxiation in its watery grave at the 'supreme day and inevitable hour', running out of the sands, still in death's struggle, the calling carcass of a boy not ready to succumb. Lifeless, the head is thrown back as if still shouting up and out, struggling against slaughter and slaying and all attempts at the final deathblow. The bloodbath boy lay back, like sheep, like pigs, like slaughterhouse bulls, cut into ribbons by the thrill-kill human race who are nothing without butchery and hatchets and vindictive cruelty. Spare none and take no prisoners! Depopulate and feel greatness! Murder and kill and cherish the skill. Laugh when the bull cries real tears, laugh when the sheep struggles at repeated stabs, laugh as the pigs dash their own brains out in preference to the massacre ahead … and this bloodbath boy did the same … kicking against entombment, punching against his urn of tarpaulin, grieving at his own funeral … the live burial which would later be termed *at rest*, when such reductions lead only to crypts and vaults and tombs without any assured rest of any kind. How very self-serving of the living to gaze upon the consigned grave spot of another and assume *at rest*. Coiled like packed supermarket pork, the short-term agony for the boy whose shape was now hardened mud, yet the sharp bones of his right hand stretched out across his chest as a final, hopeless shield at the end of a night of unforgiving beatings. Woven into the carcass were small loops of thorny blue denim – mother's hard-earned Christmas gift, divine love in sterile hell. In shadow, the terrifying weight was pulled to higher ground, and now the giant knots of tree-roots and human bone were clearly laid out as a nose-piercing fetid reek of what Shakespeare had felt when he wrote of *"the rankest compound of villainous smell that ever offended nostril"*, poor, poor Noah. Rope and leather belts of bondage clasped around the tarpaulin, and there would be no need to invest-igate further since the mechanisms of murder were all in place, and enough shock had already relieved those pre-sent of additional confirmation, as sockets empty of eyes on the thin round head of youth in decay overwhelmed our spectators. Here is the end of everything, and enough is enough. Time staggered. There came momentary pause of gentle melancholia, as if Ezra, Eliza, Nails and Justy had been taken out of themselves (or into themselves) by this misery, knowing also that none can ever escape from whatever bad deeds they have done.

"Yet … you look at this … and you still believe in some divine being? Some protector of the innocent and the good?" Nails is aim-ing directly at Ezra. *"How could this boy's murder be watched over by some supreme being who remains … unmoved? One who claims to love and care and vows reward for those who love and care?"*

"This is not the deed of God, but the deed of man," said Ezra softly.

"Yes, man made in the image of that very God … who does not show divine mercy when it is needed most. Isn't everything in God's design? Even this? Why praise him for the miracle, yet remove him from the disaster? And what had this boy ever done to anyone?" Nails was now distraught. A long and thoughtful pause

71

followed, to be broken by Ezra's request for practical action. Justy had the solution.

"I make a call to the flatheads, tell them the body is here, tell them the murderer's name, and click. What more information do they need?"

"Knowing the flatheads," said Nails, *"they'll need to know what day it is."*

"This isn't the time for flippancy," said Eliza.

"Who exactly is being flippant?" snapped Nails. *"Let them put the pieces together. Any move we make must be anonymous, and we must get away from here right this minute. All that we needed to do we've done."*

"Wait!" said Eliza in a louder whisper. She then produced a felt-tipped pen, knelt down to the torn tarpaulin, and wrote the boy's name very clearly above the upper section of his shroud: *Noah Barbelo, murdered by Dean Isaac, 1955.* From there, the four slid away.

Alone in the shower, Justy wept with ferocity. Alone in his bed, Nails wept in a malaise of torment. Enjoined, Ezra and Eliza coiled together under messy sheets, struggling to find meaning in the present.

With daybreak Dibbs stood alone on the college track.

"Where's them clowns?" asked an approaching Mr Rims, still hoping to revive what was now so very lost.

"No sign, Mr Rims," said Dibbs, with characteristically vacant aspect and considerable embarrassment. Fated to suffer, his shorts were two sizes too small, and his socks did not match.

"Hmmm?" said Mr Rims, looking easterly then westerly. *"I feel like the last one to know."*

"The last one to know what, Sir?" asked Dibbs.

"The last one to know what I don't yet know."

As if to characterize unnecessary labor, Ezra, Nails and Justy eventually made a show for a late-afternoon drill brief, even if the stiffener of dead paste at the loss of Harri disadvantaged all three. Dibbs loomed as an eager superjock of one-line jokes; flat out when the bell rang and fully ready with untiring jibberish, yet green in judgment when the whistle announced the seconds to mount and destroy all opponents.

"Yeah, I've been known to draw first blood," he joked (to smiles, of course, from no one), *"I was born with teeth, haha,"* eager as he was to disguise his all-American Neanderthal self and join the gang. It was all too much for the others who, play-by-play, burbed out like bowwow cellar dogs of faded greatness. In a sleepwalking state they somehow ran, and Rims looked on unable to convince anyone of anything yet always ready with savage Spanish Armada lash of the tongue. Enslaved, the evening continued, but nothing could show the way. It will come if it comes. The inner selves were spliced and finished, and enthusiasm constricted itself amid flashes of Harri's funeral and the wormed visions of Noah's leftover remains. Personal fallibility rose and … luck has an opposite. The bomb-burst had died, and Dibbs' conversational tone (for, loosely, it could perhaps be termed conversation) had the grating sound of religious fanaticism – tired torrents of trapped nonsense of empty-headed principles without any evidence to point to. Having let go of everything, Ezra now felt shelled and destroyed, and

Dibbs (such a child still … at risk of degrading all children) was determined to not be outdone by his own inability. Nails yawned. It was done with. The Nineteenth Hole seemed too far away in stunning sunlight, and bullwhacker Rims interrupted a bunch start.

"There is absolutely no doubt in my mind," he chewed, *"that the horse, if not the barn itself, has bolted,"* and with that he spat.

Three heads bowed solemnly as Rims revved up for further hell-driver analysis – no part of which the boys would wish to hear. Rims clambered aboard his soapbox and the grand performance began.

*"We search in life for that one race that sums everything. Well, keep searching. As they lower your cold-meat body into the ground, keep searching still. Your time could be devoted to far better things. Knitting, for example. Historians of track and field need watch you no longer. I need a stiff drink and a long sleep, or a long drink and a stiff sleep. I knew the end would come soon, but I didn't think it would come before the actual race began. At least I now realize how pointless it is trying to force things. You are all disqualified, your timings are punishable by death, and I watch your slackness in torture. If you are serious athletes then my mother is an astronaut, and you'll be sorry to hear that my mother is no astronaut. You should be forced to live face down in your own feces, as you probably do any way, if only for general identification purposes. I will be happy enough just to survive this. If I were religious, I'd pray. I could apply the lash, but why waste the lash? Now I see why some people laugh at F-Troop – not laughing **with** it but laughing **because of** it. You've been lavish with promise for so long yet now you backslide like factory-farmed pigs with no choice, pigs whose primal screams ignite no humane response from their human killers. I have watched an orgy of scared rabbits today, and Dibbs here had his harrier best at hand for all of youze. But the way through is*

barred. Close your eyes and try to recall all your previous numbers and opportunism. I now bear witness of your royal crapness. I see how Harri's death has inflicted drastic damage, and I'm enough of a humanist to feel sorrow, but you ought to be sportsmen enough to answer any challenge. You are no longer fit for consideration or even for human gaze. You are not a team. You'd get kicked out of bed. I take leave of absence. I am now very firmly a non-believer and I change my religion, the correct word for which is apostasy. You are the source of my panic and I shall let it go with some peace regained. I am free."

At this moment, Nails snorted a bull's charge and fell into Rims by planting a bashed belt that poked the rim of the chin, a non-zinger that lolloped rather than Sunday-punched, as Rims calmly avoided the noisy rustle of the oncoming slug which, in any event, hurt Nails' fist far more than it cut up Rims. The purged Nails bent over in pain and humiliation, whilst Rims stood passively puritan, the understanding gagman of unhurtable Purple Heart. His calm was impressive.

"A gallant display, Nails, but you have shown me, once again, that I should expect nothing better from you. Goodbye."

"Say … what!" jumped Dibbs, the dreams that money can't buy slipping through his fingers.

"The bad and the sad events of recent days have stripped your spirits. I see it all now just by standing here and looking at you. Sadness fleshes out … and out … and out. You are pretending and you look pale. You are crippled by the way you look and move just as much as by whatever you say. Self-floggers are of no interest to me – I've been around those people all of my life and they bore me senseless. You've just joined them. You've got to want it, and you don't, so you won't get it. Determination is not talent." Rims ran on overdrive.

"I thought you'd said goodbye?" said Nails, nursing his hand.

"Nails. To you ... someone will always be saying goodbye ..." Rims threw his final dart. With that he walked away. The ton-of-bricks shock on the faces of Ezra and Justy registered failed nerve, a loss of vocation to Harri, and a stark overture of anger. Humiliated, the still largely unknown Dibbs twitched and then fell to the ground with his hands cradling his brain – this discouragement far too much for him to bear. Fate sealed, Ezra no longer felt like the golden-boy profiteer, and there was now no identifiable unscrupulous fire within. Never to be intimidated, Nails nonetheless knew that Rims' pitiless outburst had crassly called for denial by the boys – a denial that none had the strength to make. Love's labors lost.

The dark force of seven full days dripped by before local news reports shrieked discovery of the body in the college grounds. No responsibility fell to the godly white-washed halls of Priorswood, even as it was incorrectly announced that the corpse had lain undiscovered for 'just' five years. Since the boy had not been a Priorswood student, police assumed that the body had been dumped at the college without having any direct connection to the hallowed halls, around which an abnormally solid wall of respectability suddenly erected itself. Of course, knowing nothing, the police must always imply that they know something, whilst not actually solving any serious human problems. Local television news, meanwhile, gives a practiced air of impartial reporting but angles its wording at a pre-existing attitude towards whatever it reports. At its core its reporting must influence the moral and emotional nature of its viewers, because television news narratives always assume that every person watching is exactly the same in moral temperament and social outlook and will be sufficiently exhausted by their own private struggle that they will believe everything that they see and hear on television news. Passive goodwill is the middle line, yet the overall assumption is that television viewers themselves haven't the mental capacity to penetrate any news story, so why therefore should the actual reporters? It simply is not necessary, and as long as viewers remain tortured by worry and concern, then the news has fulfilled its contract to the human race. Torrents of horror rippled through the town, yet Noah's name – so precisely printed across his tarpaulin graveclothes – would not be mentioned. In the solemn echo-chamber of Boston's most esteemed public libraries, Eliza had investigated missing-person's files in search of Noah Barbelo, but had found nothing.

The oh-so-sudden and immediate retirement of Dean Isaac sneaked out into local newsprint, with smiles and waves following fifty years of devotional service as an impeccable educator. Still single at sixty-five years, he winked with easy conscience that he now at last had the time to find a wife – the utterly insensible assumption that a carefully preserved, pony-tailed slave might still be out there waiting, and in desperate need of Isaac's crinkled crabbiness and a new set of dishcloths. The honorary evangelist spent a pleasant Tuesday morning leaning into his flower-beds by way of benevolent inspection as they trailed the border of the small and private college garden that he considered his own since the window bay of his magisterial study squinted out across it, latticed and of deep window sills. Always fighting himself, this was where he found the light that his heart always yearned for, and where he could forget his disturbing associations, no matter how capriciously the mind dragged the fat body along. He could look suffering directly in the eye as long as that suffering was not his own, yet he was now in a terrible rush, for he had never heard of sexual presumptions in either heaven or paradise, and there were now fewer years to cram more of it in – at least as far as his capacities would allow ... as a chronicler of horror, for even at twenty years old his timing had been all wrong, and life's general rites of passage were never his. The right response from the right loved one never came, and as middle age ambushed him, Isaac still struggled to construct lost youth at the Junior Prom that never was, and the Eagle Scouts that shut him out, having no idea what to do next, throughout years and years of sexual silence. Now, in slipping maturity, he was a sorry image of the overripe drifting into life's final chapters as if they were a sandy whirlwind of death – which, in fact, they were. A solemn parley of memories filled dull Thursday evenings, but the doctor was becoming the patient, which, in his confidence game, he did not like. The pain of being jealous of the very flesh that we admire! The pain of longing to be what would never be! Life surrounds like lumbering fat, further demeaned by each racing year, slavishly chasing the unattainable. Mother knew everything yet said nothing, for to say anything was to provide oxygen. Mother died and the son lied. It would all be over soon enough, anyway, and dean of the faculty had been position enough, and it is so easy to pervert and corrupt whilst occupying the most trusted and endowed chair of academic ranks. *But oh, could there be someone one day who might make sense of me? And if it is not designed to be, then why am I able to imagine it?*

"Excuse me, Dean Isaac?" Ezra appeared, closing the heavy wrought-iron gate that led into the secret garden, and he positioned himself in Isaac's view.

"Now, you know very well that this is a private garden and you have no rightful access to it," smiled Isaac, with the gentle reproach of a kindly pastor. Ezra stepped closer still.

"Did you not hear what I've just said?" went on Isaac, with slight scientific detachment, looking about for flowers in bloom. Ezra now decided that he, too, would smile as he spoke.

"By way of some apology I should tell you that I am here to help you," he said. Isaac stiffened and stood upright, as if preparing a reprimand.

"Help me?" Isaac's smile began to dim. *"Your impertinence is about to get you into serious trouble. I know who you are — you are our little Ezra Pound, and I issue the most severe warning to you. Now, get out."*

"Before any punishment takes place I will tell you that I am perilously close to saving your soul, although after today you will never have a life of your own," said Ezra.

"A greeting-card jokester you might very well be within your own fraternity, but arty-smartiness does not impress me. I shall call the House Master at once and you will be dealt with, and let's hope that this sort of hilarity does not tempt you ever again. I do not like you, so go away." Isaac made a move towards the wrought-iron

gate, yet a small part within him knew more than he knew, and it broke down at impending sadness even if the impression of sound reason must be reinforced at all costs. This Ezra Pound obviously knew something, and was about to blab, and Isaac had no wish to hear anything at all that might prick his confidence.

"Noah Barbelo," said Ezra, *"and the orgy of cruelty that ended his life. You read about it in the newspapers, I'm sure, but this was not the first time you knew about it."*

"What has that to do with me?" Isaac's voice suddenly a thin timbre.

"You killed him. If you didn't, then make the denial in court."

"What sort of scientific hypothesis is this? You have sealed your expulsion from Priorswood with those very words, and through proper legal channels I shall make such claims of slander that will financially destroy your entire family. You are a bully-boy and your words have inflicted an unimaginable web of sorrow on your own family. I shall see to that with no difficulty. Your joke is in poor taste and I can only assume that you are dismayingly simple in intellect."

Isaac's smile was now shrewd, but the eyes were downcast.

"That is the wrong answer and the wrong reaction. You are not as sharp as I'd imagined," Ezra stood his ground.

"Who do you think you are, and what do you want from me?"

"Again, the wrong answer ... for you are now bargaining ... and as for this college, well, I shan't miss it very much ... which is immaterial anyway, since I now look with pity on your tall and lonely figure. Your shoulders are tired and your eyes are transfixed with terror. The smile is frightened. All you possess are remnants of snobbery ... which is not enough to save you now, even though you have learned over many years how to sound right even when wrong. That's

the entire point of people like you, isn't it? Confidence and composure automatically qualifies you as being accurate and correct … the mannerly way of getting out of things … the meticulous measuring of words … all done the conventional way, phenomenally evil."

Isaac quickly looked cautiously to the left, and then to the right, and sensing a clear coast he whacked the back of his right fist across Ezra's face so violently that Ezra, as solid as he was, dropped to the ground. Looking up at Isaac he could see the polluted agent of trust sliding into barbaric mode, loosening his belt – for what reason, Ezra could only guess – and Ezra hastily stumbled to his feet and collected himself whilst wisely moving back towards the gate. *"There is nothing you can do, and there is no chance of rest for you now, for I am not alone in knowing what I told you today … and although I stand alone in this garden, you are, in fact, surrounded."* Ezra fled the scene, and some things are indeed too much for the human mind as his final fleeting glimpse of the Isaac countenance caught a bigoted face teetering upon breakdown, God or no God.

Whilst the muddled media frenzied about with expertly worried brows over the Watergate cover-up, adding their own fake fury and mania to turbulence and greed (as if actually surprised at any wrong-doing in high places), the cosmos, never to be halted, laughed at its audience of illiterates and wound its way on. Earth, after all, was either an asylum or a prison cell compared to the greater universe. Most Americans were still primarily afraid of the weather, and required infantile reassurances of comfort … as Saigon falls. From Watergate to the crappy hatched *Wheel of Fortune* the system worked well as long as the people thought abjectly of themselves and as long as free enquiry remained impossible for the average American, to whom mushroom-shaped clouds and the stoutest of bibles kept the populace either shriveled or stoned, with only the stars above to determine our destinies. The frightening mentality of the daily press went on and on, unsure of the true age of the sun, yet condemning to death anyone who enjoyed marijuana. The strong are always barbaric, and the finest working models of American society are still those who would never dare question firmness, strictness, Christianity, or the untouchable food and farming industries. Correctional facilities, or jails, were overstuffed with the hapless poor – whose poverty was their own fault and a crime in itself, yet prisons were absent of errant lawyers, wayward bankers or blundering judges who had failed society. It could seem fair to assume that the police existed only in order to protect the rich from the poor without a slip of evidence to suggest otherwise. Bible belters could not loosen their belts; America will burn in hell should it fail to uphold beliefs for which none had evidence.

"This is International Women's Year," muttered Eliza as she slouched across Ezra's bed. *"Only this year, of course … next year we all return to our pens … as in places of confinement, not writing materials. Could you imagine International Men's Year? The very words are ridiculous … yet apparently not for women. We're right up there with the Year of the Pig."*

"Well," Professor Ezra began, *"England apparently has its first leader of a political party who is female."*

"No," said Eliza, *"England has its **last** female party leader. She's already a token woman … saying she's not a feminist … umm, I wonder how she broke through those gates, then … on the strength of her featherweight boxing, I suppose. I hate womb-men like that*

... they just can't wait to be one of the boys ... and just watch, if she becomes prime minister she won't hire any women into her government. Why do I even care? I mean, just look at her face – it's all there in plain anguish ... cheat the poor ... "

Suddenly Ezra broke into a heavy sob, and Eliza threw her arms around him. *"It's all too much,"* he said.

"Margaret Thatcher? I know. But politics only attracts that kind of prejudiced cipher," she offered, soaking into Ezra. *"We never have Anne Sexton or James Baldwin types running the country. They'd make far too much sense."*

"No, not Margaret Hatchet ... Everything here ... the boy ... Isaac ... the non-tournament ..."

"Her name is Thatcher ... although, I dunno ... you could be right when you say Hatchet. Just look at that boneless face ... if ever an engine of grief... Look, I wouldn't worry about the tournament. It's already unwon. It's gone, and ... haven't you noticed? More important things have replaced it. What's so impressive about running along clutching a little-boy baton? Children are starving to death all over the world ... government officials are having enlightened activists bumped off ... dictators are slaughtering the people of their own country ... two billion loving animals a year are being butchered in concentration camps ... chained alongside their sisters and their mothers as they wriggle and struggle for a compassion alien to the human spirit ... and you're worried about sports results?" Eliza rainstormed her anger down on Ezra. *"Have you ever watched the TV news, and listened to all of their scare-tactic propaganda ... every story designed to frighten you, scare you off, make you feel small, make you feel alarmed yet hopeless ... and then – bam! – 'and now we have some sports news', as if this ought to counterbalance all the shit that's happening in the world. What an insult to the victims of mass slaughter and war and murder to have it followed by sports*

news. *How does sports news qualify to be mentioned alongside the murderous insanity of this planet? Why are sports even thought to be a national subject? I don't know anyone who plays golf or Australian rugby. Why should I care? Also, you don't ever see a story on the news that tells you how you can rally against or object or contest or halt or call to arms ... or how you can dispose of corrupt govern-ments ... no! They just tell how dreadful it is and how endangered you are and how nothing can be done to make change."* Eliza scoffs, ignited by her own words.

"Well, why do you watch the TV news, then?" Ezra was soothing.

"I don't, but I know it's there and I know it never changes because the object is to appear to inform people whilst actually telling them nothing. Politicians are the same. They are trained to appear to answer questions without actually parting with information. If you're in politics your main skill must be concealing the truth, and that's all you ever need to do. It's almost comical ... this possession of power ... this preoccupation with appearing dangerous. We, my lover, my friend, are their enemies ... we, the people ... never to be told how easy it is to get rid of dictators. I mean, when I was at school I wasn't taught how to deal with the police, or how to deal with any judicial authority. Were you?"

"No."

"Why not?"

"Because both have less power than we'd imagine and they rely on our ignorance in order to keep their jobs."

"They have hardly any powers. I remember my uncle being cross-examined and being told how ignorance of the law is no excuse, and he said 'your law is not my law,' and the judge extended his sentence just for saying those words. The judge had no interest in what my uncle meant because ... um, well, let's not get into the wanton buggery of

84

*judicial thuggery … yet, how sad it must be to wake up and to fall asleep dreaming about violations and violators and courts and slapping people down … this pretense of goodness and godliness enforcing law by any means and with such churchgoing disapproval intent on jailing the entire population … getting the black kids hooked so that they're too dazed and harmless and spaced. You've got to hand it to Congress, they know how to disable their opposition. The Narcotics Department puts the drugs on the streets, the kids get hooked, the youth are criminalized and the state retains control of everyone's movements. I thought the Nazis **lost** the war? Arrest the police!"*

Angela Davis looked down from the wall.

"I've got to do it for Harri," started Ezra, *"I've got to get this tournament together. It can't slide away. I've got to pull Rims back."*

"But Rims has quit eight times!" shouted Eliza, *"he's gone!"*

"His no doesn't always mean no. I can get another day's grace from him."

"You talk about him like he's the Pope," sniffed Eliza.

"Oh he's much more important than that."

Reinsman Rims called everyone together for a final crack at the track. He was in his best charioteer mood with his coachy-coachy tones all a-shower of stats and this and thats, overages and averages. *"Why – do – I – even – bother?"* he had begun, *"and for that matter, why do you? I have far better things to do. There's Japanese golf on channel 38 today and I could be, well, I could be …"*

"Japanese?" stuck in Nails.

Dibbs suddenly laughed far too loudly, like a booby-hatch inmate.

"What's so funny?" asked Rims in a boggled drawl. Dibbs' expression reversed to a frostbitten frown. Though their teal kits and tackle and traps were impressive, the stringy squad also looked very much the unfit outfit, a varsity of pity platooned in gloom.

"Alright, Bobby Unser, what exactly is going on?" Rims directed to Ezra. *"The IAAF would rightly shoot me dead if I presented you as roadworthy. The National Federation of Athletics Associations wouldn't be much interested either. What is going on? Tell Telly all about it."*

"There are worms mating in the hollowed sockets of Harri's eyes," wheezed Ezra.

"And lucky he is to have us mourn him. There are graves deserted all over the world. There were healthy young Polish women who died revealing nothing to Nazi soldiers. Most lives come to a pointless end, a scrap of paper bearing a hastily scribbled name stuffed inside a jam-jar, and no death ever stopped the world. Life's sharp corners come to us all, and don't think you'll be excluded. If I had the gift of adequate words I would harshly tell you that nothing has happened to Harri that does not await the rest of us. Your time will come. Or would you rather curl up and die today? Your end is not yet, and that, I'm afraid, is all that life is about, so stop thinking about how things ought to be and … just look around you. Faith is a very precious component, wrest from it what you can, this day is for you, and you'll wish for its return in time, so shut your mouth and set an example to oblivion because it's been unable to nab you as yet. Feel unhappy? Work it off. You fail, you die. Brim with school pride and generate pep for the team, otherwise dry your little button-eyes and get your cold, dead legs in action."

Lynette Fromme sat entranced in her private quarters, debunked yet determined, as she premeditated making a run at the assassination of President Gerald Ford. Intrigue fed dreams with blitzkrieg schemes and Fromme would liquidate with one pulled trigger as her chartered course, calling out with a shootist's plea for cleaner air for the people of America, for healthy water for the people of America, and for respect for animals – each apparently amiss on the busy Ford agenda. In other rooms, Sara Jane Moore also shaped Ford's neutralization by taking him out in much the same way; a heavy date for a president who was about to meet the people – or two, at least, but minus the usual pre-assigned photo-op flimflam fakery. How do the people get through to the man of the people? Well, they don't – not if he can help it. Both hit-women would coincidentally present arms in this coming September of 1975, although on different days, and even though both would be inches away from Ford's brisket pecs the firearms of both Fromme and Moore would bedevil the hunters in a bewitchingly jinxed fashion, and they would both fail to waste the president. Both women would be imprisoned for far longer terms than the benevolent gods had allotted for Gerald Ford to live out the remainder of his natural life on planet Earth; their actions so astonishing that even Ford's natural death did not allow Fromme and Moore the freedom to at least dance on his grave. Thus, they remained in jail for attempting to kill someone whom they not only did not kill, but someone who was in any event no longer alive … as they languish in prison as a reminder to all that the law makes up its own details as it goes along, and that society cannot threaten those in power by whom society feels threatened. Politicians marvel at the submissive gullibility of the electorate, and the hang-hungry judges of America remained beagle-beaked on their benches; blindfolded Father Time always ready to throw the book and run up the flagpole.

Prior to all of this commotion our pure-hearted and devotional track boys finally saw June loom as the deadliest month, as life caught up with fantasy (or perhaps the other way around), a gloomy coincidence that no one could have predicted. There was suddenly no sign of a forgiving Jehovah, and our superior boys were now inferior hangdogs fully absent of the divine light of reason. Noah Barbelo's name had slipped from print as an embarrassingly timed discovery that had been inefficiently investigated and then flicked away with easy conscience. Had Noah been Naomi, perhaps the hot-pants turn-on might have sweet-toothed the press into a more aroused cruise mode, but it was rarely admitted that such off-base sex attacks could possibly befall boys such as Noah, and thus the media struggled with the language required to describe what they could have outlined with such impressive oomph and glitz had Noah been a fluffy girl. The dense and insensible Dean Isaac spun further black magic, with his carefully orchestrated retirement plans walloped across local newspapers, bearing witless bylines accompanying excited shots of Isaac infatuated with his own reflection as he wore his coat on his shoulders in cloak fashion, and waving confidently to the world beyond the lens that made flesh and then created truth, and into which the entire universe peered back from the other side – with no voice. Smiling with pork-fat contentment, heroically soaked in elitist sanctification, Isaac was ready for a new dawn – one which, many years ago, Noah Barbelo had no right to claim and no reason to expect. Might successfully impinges upon right. Although the police had been anonymously and eloquently tipped off, Noah's name tip-toed into cautious page-twelve scrutiny minus any link to Isaac, and minus any journalistic penetration into the full cause of death, for life is too short to stretch the imagination further than necessary; boy-sex murder not worthy of the peepshow circus automatically unwound for the sexploitative girl-sex murder. The boy had lived quietly with his now-absent mother, both of them lost in the greyness of shaded side streets of no influence, no family, no useful links to the icy judiciary, all of which presented a perfect concoction for horndog Isaac and his protected pederast wish-fulfilment. Are the lowly and lonely likes of Noah ever a courtroom success? No. Did title and unflappable wealth protect Dean Isaac's necrophilic lust from moral investigation? Well, of course. We are spared the details of precisely how Noah Barbelo died, or why whoever killed him considered the boy unfit for further sunlight. Death shifts, my little buddha, my little buddha, and how soon an old story just does not matter.

Confused all over again, Ezra stood sealed in his teal college kit and waited for whatever was to come just to get on with the irascible business of coming.

"Let's tear up the track!" bounced dogtrot Dibbs, *"let's out-strip the wind!"* he belched, *"let's make some knots!"* the hot air hooted on, as Dibbs burst into a high-pitched yelp that only the sexually secure male might dare accept of himself … *"Let's give it the gun!"* the launch went on, exhausting everyone around him, who could only glare at the bouncing, beheaded mockery before them.

89

"Dibbs?" said Nails very softly.

"Yes, Sir!" suck-ass replied.

"Have the common decency to die soon. Consider your friends," said Nails, the words hitting precisely as they should. *"Three's company, four's a crowd."*

"OK!" Dibbs jumped back, embarrassed to be misled by over-confidence. He then visibly shrank several inches.

Spot starter Ezra rose courageously from the starting block with a trimly sprint to second baseman Nails – a tight and shipshape acceleration, flat-out throttle of speed, with quickening cannonball blast giving a confident hand-over to third bagger Justy, who gripped the baton all ataunto, with the old glory rising like the lash of a whip at the starboard tip of a mid-storm ship losing its grip, as wide-open spikes thundered along as they ate up the track and to never look back or to give a rat's ass … back at 'cha, back at 'cha, back at 'cha … and should I never make love again let murder and rust befall me now and let those I love abort and die … but just let me win, let me win, let me win! My legs! My legs! My life! In your face, in your face, in your face, lover do I never need as long as I have these that send me like the wind … the bullet of Justy as a hell-driver flyer with a disciplined land into Dibbs' dry hand, and the new corner man faced the home straight with power-hitter grunts and Bunkie pluck as the bilge-free body speedballed with stirred stumps to beat the devil with scorch and sizzle and unfortunate dribble and snappy like crazy he somersaulted with pitching motion into a ferocious belly-flop tumble of a sprawled pratfall – face to the gravel, each limb slithered like snowslide subsidence. In slow motion, Ezra, Nails and Justy watched the concluding pantomime with all of its outlines now clear … and there is some suffering, after all, from which no strength can be drawn. Dibbs lay in tears on his back on the track, the baton flung somewhere towards hell, damnation and Cleveland.

"There's a coffin out there with your name on it," leaned in no-mercy Nails. *"I will bury you."*

Dibbs cried louder, *"People are allowed to make mistakes!"*

"People, yes, but that excludes you," Nails spat.

"When exactly did you die?" came Justy, leaning over the incapacitated turd. Dibbs cried louder still.

"You are vegetable dip, you are a fucken hairball … I have nothing more to say to you. I'll save all of my hatred for your funeral – which we shall all enjoy." Nails could not stop himself, and therefore didn't attempt to. Rims was soon on the spot, and, as always, he began his rag-chewing speech.

"Such days as these only exist for people who are thankful. I am no such person. This is the lowest point of my entire life. I have wasted a full hour when I could have been somewhere else getting something uncomfortably pierced. It's different for all of you, of course, because you can all at least plead insanity … with your faces like slipped discs, who would doubt? But some of us have good reputations, just as, as you've displayed, some are bagged by PMS days. Quite beyond the power of words to describe! But let me try! I have never before seen a relay team getting in the way of their own race – with only themselves on the track. No explanation is possible for this. I very suddenly have an old soul. What's worse is … I don't actually mind. Today we have new meaning to the word tragedy, and, I don't quite know how to put this, but," and then he paused an intake of deep breath in preparation for his final, deeply emphatic *"goodbye"*, which came with assurance, and there it was. With the bitterness of it all Rims moved quickly

away from the funeral pyre, as he had done so many times, smaller and smaller as he hunched his way into the distance and into this story's history. Our three soldiers symbolically ripped off their college singlets.

"A-ban-don ship!" said Ezra, with bite.

"Ske-daddle!" sighed Nails, with hate in his voice.

Cold-bloodedly they left Dibbs sobbing with his face buried in his hands, unable to stand up from where fate had plonked him. Let it all now pass ... and it shall. Free of tournament deadlines, all faith came to an end, and had always been something of a problem to begin with. Trapped, they were now free, and the team died out with a sad awareness that they would not be remembered for what they had been in those glory days of late summer afternoons when reward outstripped sacrifice and the sun shone on the young sons of smiles and sardonic doggerel, shaped into a supreme fitness design with the world at their feet (since their feet were their world). It was all done with, now – that playful time of sarcastic kicks, sunny natured treading of the pitch ... teasing girls when sex comes next. Hearts may die but these bones are immortal ... the striding man of satiric gait, non-timid he with all in place, as blessed as the best. More tears to be cried as all three stood at Harri's symbolic stone, he barely settled in his grave as a forgotten saint for whom no more hope could help. Claims of protection rushed through the boys of hearty hugs ... a substitute for closer affection, as yet unmastered. So easy to say 'I love you' when the warrior cannot respond, and is now a composite of clay for mighty maggot and slightish mite.

"I love you, maestro," stammered Justy in that far too easy

way of not quite saying much, staring at the chipped words on stone which sharpened the need for praise and regret. *"I said it before and I repeat it now."* Yet the before was to he of unassailable youth, and the now was to the perished life below – surrendered to the way of all flesh and gathered to one's fathers, yet his laughter rang on – those strong teeth and pinkish lips. How could they ever be less than what they once were? What divine creationist could be evil enough to make them less, having crafted them in the first place? Why not the joy of ugly into beauty? The porky child becomes the marvel of steaming richness. Why must decay have the final say, and who so decided? Rhapsodically the boys linked their arms around one another's shoulders as boulders of lamenting love, so much of Harri in all of them. No claims made on the body, but the poetry of true friendship looked down on the juvenility of mannishly boyish fumblings which could only appear in so many juvenescent permutations before it all becomes so predictably cubbish and the grown man appears ungrown after all, and vulnerable and unfinished; virginal at 50, fallow at 60. Unsown, the *I-ex-love-you* yatter becomes a nightclub act of yesteryear gags, a bed forever too neatly made, tripped up by dated 20th Century Fox 1940s dialogue, as 25-year-olds who weren't even born at the time when you were already sick of it all now looked over at you and smiled a nod of compassionate pity. The toil and task of avoiding non-accomplishment is no more powerful than in the sexual edges. Labor and effort can lead nowhere, dreams unconsummated, the end of an unfinished life. To die open-ended, sexually overlooked, non-consummation tittering its execution, you are discharged from pain as you close your eyes, as, like all bacteria, we die away, a falling with none to catch. Ezra, Nails and Justy felt a love for each other that prospered without the sexual, or found prosperity precisely because the sexual did not make propositions. But as their spirit forever struggles with the flesh, who is to say that their closeness was not in fact a liberating scream of the intensely sensual? Does *anybody* know? Can *anybody* control the inestimable effects of touch? Their outcome was fortunate and felt certain to last. Erotic at times, yes, but safely unsaid. Are we always waiting for life to stop? If you give someone the yes or no option, isn't it true that they will always choose the no?

At Ledger's Bar the day splintered with the sudden appearance of an over-made-up Tracey, phenomenally top-heavy and modernly unfashionable. She had once found herself harnessed in Harri's arms, and thus her dial-twisting way of talking began.

"I don't know how to deaden the pain," she said to Ezra and Nails, *"and I assume there isn't a way. I pull myself together and then suddenly I'm drowning again. I'll have a straight gin. I pull myself together and then I'm drowning again. I'll have a straight gin. I've tried to pull myself together but then I find I'm drowning all over again. It isn't fair. I'll have a straight gin. I've tried to pull myself together – everyone knows that, but then I find I'm ... "* suddenly it was Ezra and Nails who were drowning. *" ... and even when I finally pull myself together ... I'll have a straight gin it isn't fair."*

On the television that blared ridiculously loudly above the bar Muhammad Ali yapped his fired soul of rascal fury at the announcement of his future marketplace boxing theatrics with Joe Frazier. Ali, a showbusiness show-off combining the expected lack of respect and the full

94

stage-show dramatics with the illusory importance of what would be, in fact, no more than a glorified shoving match – the best promise a grown man can make to the world; how easy to kill, how queasy to kiss. There are too many secrets in nature. Singing voices are love, but a professional fight pulls in millions of dollars, whereas a similar scrap on the street ends in arrest and public humiliation and the almighty godliness of the ever-sacred cash fine to the court's quite immoral advantage. There is no financial gain from the street-corner bust-up, and since money turns the world, the courts rake in as much of it as they can at the expense of human misfortune, *hahaha*. Oh, where would the established elite be without the have-nots! No trapped raccoons to fleece of their coats, and none to make the anarchic rich feel immune to argument. Meanwhile, governor Ronald Reagan flashes a crooked and frozen ice-box smile as he throws his metaphorical hat into the presidential race ring – an ideal antidote to everything now visible on the streets of America. Reagan has no time for black power, women's rights, gay liberation, animal rights, anti-war rallies or student demonstrations. He contrasts all of the exciting changes that made America new again, and he offers old-fashioned power-politics, the type of which must always keep a profitable war on the go … everything old (including himself) sold off like fake insurance to the all-powerful conglomerate America of *Bonanza*, a rich and expertly presented daily television drama where cow-rustling Ben Cartwright lives handsomely with his three sons (none of whom share one single gene, since all three are of different mothers, and, magically, all three mothers are either dead or hidden behind studio curtains).

Throughout fourteen years of constant transmission, the entire cast of *Bonanza* wears the same outfits, unchanging with each episode, the hayseed symbolism not lost on conservative Americans who cherish unchanging times and unchangeable minds. Since the Cartwrights are wealthy upcountry landowners, it might be wondered why they feel undeserving of a second set of clothing, yet viewers are unable to puzzle at how Little Joe Cartwright's waist-size remains the same at age 34 as it had been when he started the show at age 20. His lilac pants are never discarded, or even once removed. Deeper still, the three very adult Cartwright brothers possess a natural virility and capable masculinity in the hog-wild west yet they are childishly answerable to their father in a family duty that transcends simple respect, and instead lurches towards an almost perverted hereditary Christian bondage; and although deity Ben Cartwright had fathered three sons from three women who had usefully dissolved into tumbleweed, his three strapping sons themselves do not reproduce and almost never pair off for passionate romance. Passion, in fact, is unseen at their backwoods Ponderosa ranch, and the sexual act (clearly enjoyed by their father) does not pass on to the frontier sons, not even in the prairie dustbowl of the 1860s, where there really cannot be very much to do to ignite happiness in the average human animal. There would never be any reference to the sexual act in *Bonanza*, and although the four men live openly and intelligently together, no heart-to-heart or tittle-tattle prittle-prattle ever touches upon the workings of the very male bodies in which all four struggle to live, and certainly there is no man's-country evidence of the Cartwrights being in possession of genitalia, even though every conceivable global problem befalls them at the Ponderosa ranch, causing them to do virtually anything other than discuss their own physicality (which, in itself, manifests as a ruthless punishment). As with most parents, Ben Cartwright demands that his sons be younger copies of himself, and they comply without question, for they are indeed good sons. *Bonanza*, though, is TV evangelism surviving well into the rabble-rousing America of Ronald Reagan, whose impish wife gazes up at him as he gives each after-dinner lecture – she with the fawnish face of a dying child who is unable to exist for herself as a totality. Laura Bush will much later adopt the same gaseous and servile soap-opera affectation when her own husband becomes America's latest Ben Cartwright, and she, too, will proudly gaze upwards into his eyes as he delivers yet another hellfire illiterate's public address that is almost always obsessed with killing people. Although Reagan in himself is a past event, he becomes current in the politics of 1975 because America has always feared the future and will forever seek a familiar if untrustworthy 'type' (with whom one at least knows where one stands) rather than seek someone who might glow or advance America's global popularity (the purity of which is in any case not to be questioned). What is happening on the streets of America, and the stormy shouts of the new youth who demand to be allowed to be what they are and were born to be, provided Reagan with a deep commitment to opposing the people, his policies as cruel as the Church. Like all world leaders, Reagan could only be confirmed by the terror he instilled in the people of his country, for this makes for the appearance of solid supervision in a society with no wish to evolve. Whilst animals in packs care for each other, feed each other, share resources and call warnings to each other, the human race thrives only on self-interest. The more targeted approach of Reagan comes directly off the set of *Bonanza*, and, persistently unable to remember his lines, someone in charge of history will categorize him as a 'great communicator' ... and it really is that easy and as equally demented.

Ezra's shadowy face falls into Eliza's breasts as they both curl half in yet half out of a sleeping-bag. The basement is always free of bothersome family fuss, and it is here that Ezra and Eliza are free to convey tender generosity without fear of intrusion into their lovers' bunker. The cyclone cosiness of this underground crib, with its teen-crap depository of big-box storage and a battered and blinking portable television set as it nags and nags and nags at low volume, was at least our fledglings' nest of snuggle and nestle, settled as they were watching the wrecked tension of the nightly news.

"Who ... or what ... is Ronald Reagan?" asked Ezra, stricken with exhaustion.

"He's the strongest of the weakest," says Eliza, in a corny cornball American pretzel voice, *"and they says he'll be our next president, which means he* **shall** *be our next president ... because they says he will, and civilization runs its full-bellied porky course ... Malcolm X, Martin Luther King, James Baldwin ... ssh, they just didn't have what it takes when pitted against Ronald Reagan, Lordy no! Civil rights? Bullcrap! Social justice? Praise me, no! Angela Davis? Bless my heart alive! Gloria Steinem? Bullcrap! Bullcrap? Bullcrap! If you're black, get back! Greenpeace? Terrorist watch! Rosa Parks? Nuisance! Dick Gregory? Social pest! Cesar*

Chavez? Headcase! American Civil Liberties Union? Whacko! Separate but equal? Goofy! Hooray for oil, oil, oil! Hooray for State terrorism! Commercial whaling! Nuclear bombs! Deforestation! Toxic waste! Yee-haw! Arrest Joan Baez and Buffy Sainte-Marie … political prisoners you-know-where-and-when! Bob Dylan?"

"*Er, point taken –*" cut in Ezra, but Eliza continued anyway …

"*Ronald Reagan … now there's the marrow of the American bone … he'll bomb Japan just to return a very private favor … and all American cops will make you beg … in the land of the free and the home of the brave.*"

"*When will there be a president that the people actually like?*" asked a now-dozing Ezra.

"*It's never necessary to go that far. As long as big business bankers like him, he's in. You don't actually believe that public votes are correctly counted, do you?*"

"*Of course not.*"

"*On appearance alone no one would vote for Ronald Reagan.*"

"*That must be a hairpiece?*"

"*No, the hair is real, but the rest of him isn't.*" Eliza then began to reflect wistfully. "*I remember as a child we would always say how politics is boring, and then you're led to believe that this is a somewhat unintelligent thing to say, and you are told that politics is life, and so on. But it's the politics of politics that is boring, not the mechanisms of human issues … but because you know very well that only slippery people can become successful in politics … disingenuous shitbags … yet never, ever anyone who cares about the people, or who listens to the people, or whom we could …*"

"*… call 'darling'?*" Ezra piped up.

At this, Eliza and Ezra rolled together into the one giggling snowball of full-figured copulation, screaming and shouting as they playfully bit and pulled at each other in a dangerous and clamorous rollercoaster coil of sexually violent rotation with Eliza's breasts barrel-rolled across Ezra's howling mouth and the pained frenzy of his bulbous salutation extenuating his excitement as it whacked and smacked its way into every muscle of Eliza's body except for the otherwise central zone. Both fell awkwardly off the bed, each tending to their own anguish yet still laughing an impaired discomfort of giggles whilst curving into a hunched disadvantage.

"Cojones are not the most useful accouterments at times like these," groaned Ezra.

"Yes, I know. I traded mine in at a Tupperware party. I came away with a lovely butter-boat that was far more useful and much admired in New Bedford."

Man looked at woman and woman looked at man with all the difficult dissimilarities and inequalities and arguments and varying obstacles now – and only now – harmonizing so beautifully as they unflatteringly coiled in carnage on the coarse basement rug.

"The reason why I love you the best is because I don't mind in the least if you see me at my worst," said Eliza, with cushioned voice.

"Well hopefully it doesn't get any worse than this, because my stomach just couldn't take it ..." and their fiendishly loving wrestle began once again, rolling across the floor as hot-tempered enthusiasts of lustful joy as both adorers' bodies did their sexual staccato heaving and barging into place, nothing forbidden, heartbeats uneven, the mind as naked as the body, weakened by exertion, only to shockingly lock with a halt at the astride legs of Sammy, younger brother to Ezra, as he quietly stood with satisfied slyness watching

the debauched display of sensuous pleasure at the sweetness of living by seizing the initiative.

"*Well, now!*" said Sammy, looking down at the creature-comfort nudity. Sammy smirked with blackmailer's cunning. "*I have never quite been this close to roadkill before,*" he said, deliberately pursing his lips voluptuously.

"*But you **are** roadkill,*" said Ezra. Sammy raised his extortionist's eyebrows.

"*This will cost you,*" he said, but no sooner had the words formed when Ezra sprang to his feet with clenched fist ready to hit the spot and Sammy darted from the basement in fear of his life.

During this same evening Nails and Justy kept discreet watch across the street from the Helen Earth Drag and Supper Club, from where Dean Isaac emerged at 11 p.m., after the dragged-up machete cabaret of Wilma Dickfit, Ann Shandy and Connie Lingus had reduced a Judy Garbage audience to puddles of giggles. Living his own death, afraid of the future, belching at will, through it all Isaac could only hear Noah Barbelo whispering, whispering, calling and calling into Isaac's inner ear. The club valet, named Chesty Normous, was most forthcoming and handed Isaac a set of car keys, and the flashy Maserati swirled from kerbside and home to the cosy ecstasy of Isaac's inner climate, where all of his dreams were perfectly legal and a certain emotional dryness could only be served and saved by the love of books by authors long-since withered in overgrown graves. In militant action Nails and Justy followed intently in the battered El Camino, the suffering of Noah Barbelo having transformed their hearts into procurable, securable mission that, by reason of its being, meant that Noah might no longer be in torment. The surety of the positive mind! Noah may very well still win!

The world panics along on its inexplicable course, and the loss of the June tournament freed all three boys from the disenchanted pressure of what, after all, had only ever been a dissoluble pastime. Sport was only sport, for if it were religion it would instead be called religion. Noah's murder had united Nails, Justy and Ezra – and even Eliza. Far more than the slave-trade barks of Mr Rims, or the gesture of a juggler's trophy (which, in any case, they were not unquestionably certain to win). At the impressive home of Isaac, electronic gates threw open their arms as lord and master's Maserati sailed in and moved quickly up the darkened driveway. But the gate's mechanism paused and closed too slowly to notice the darting figures of Nails and Justy neatly nipping through the narrowing gap as they systematically launched their bodies sideways into shrubbery like high-jump masters swooping backwards over the raised bar. Even so, there would be no squandering of time, and as Isaac fumbled and fiddled about with door keys both boys allowed the graveled driveway stones underfoot to announce their arrival behind the slightly swaying fruit-fondler. He turned and hazily examined their determined, jockeyed temperament.

"Well, well," beamed Isaac, *"and there was I anticipating another night of that infernal Vicki Carr long player … 'It must be him / It must be him / Oh my dear God / It must be **him**' … you'd think the wretched thing would just answer the phone, wouldn't you? God forbid she be surprised."*

"We noticed you at the club," said Nails.

"I hardly think so. They'd never let you in wearing those clothes.

Which is much to their loss, I might add," eased Isaac, clearly a professional in situations of seduction.

"No, we're from the kitchen. We understand you enjoy company from time to time," Justy offered, but not without some slight nerve deserting him. This particular ruse did not come easily to Justy, whose intended beating of Isaac might squeeze out a full confession yet could also quite messily lead to Isaac's death.

"Yes," wheezed Isaac, *"I'm prehistoric in that respect. Occasionally I even pay hard cash for it, as one must when the law decides that there is nothing natural about your nature. Nothing could have created what I am, apparently. I am beyond science. Well, we are fortunate enough to know more than whatever it was they thought they knew during the Bronze Age, aren't we? If God got it right from the beginning then surely he managed to get me right, too? I'm not a social coincidence. I look at young men such as yourselves, and that really is enough for me. Why the newspapers still get in such an amazed tizzy about it all is quite ridiculous, isn't it? You'd think they'd be used to it by now, wouldn't you? There's no record of Jesus getting hot under the collar over the girl next door, is there? But he certainly had his men around him. But then, he didn't write anything down … which was very remiss of him. Even to this day some people think that he actually wrote the Bible. He didn't write anything at all. Funny, isn't it? Please come inside."* Isaac spoke with a soft confidence.

Once inside, all three settled into the main reception room, with its elegant calmness of prosperity and contentment the likes of which Nails and Justy may have noticed in the films of Douglas Sirk but nowhere else (for it existed nowhere else). They eased into the restful comfort of Rockefeller richness; the buffed luxury of W. Buffett;

mounted paintings of interest to Onassis, or Hughes, or Vanderbilt, or Rothschild ... or perhaps not, but these were the jittery thoughts of Nails and Justy as tall glasses of vodka were thrust into their hardbitten hands and a settled Isaac tinkered by the drinks cabinet and prattled on – more for his own amusement than that of others.

"My personal fortunes are of considerable interest to many people – myself included, I should add. I once met an ill-tempered monarch in Europe, and I explained to him that I had no interest in the female form, and he found this to be far too confusing for the human mind to comprehend, or, at least, his own mind struggled with it – he said as much, anyway, and then I knew I was speaking to an illiterate. Being a monarch, of course, he felt he should secure full control over the thoughts of others. He was very religious and therefore completely racist and everything-ist, and he seemed preoccupied with punishment and hell damnation upon anyone who disagreed with him ... you know how they are. The natural order is the one that essentially suits them, and they consider execution far too comfortable an end for people who don't share their very private lusts. 'Don't shove it in our faces,' he warned me, and I thought, well, you've been married four times yourself ... shoving it in our faces over and over again. I've lived with intolerance all of my life, of course, which is why I terrify ignorant people ... since most of them have never had cause to use their brains. The Church is obsessed with everlasting punishment, or forgiveness, and I could never understand why. It's not enough to commit yourself to God – but you are quite unfairly obliged to commit yourself every single day, hour after hour. With every small action you have to keep letting him know how much you love and honor him. Why can't you just tell him once and be done with it? Why does he need to know every thirty minutes? Doesn't he believe anyone who ever says it? I don't want some dreadful priest forgiving

me as I lie there in a coma, with no new things lurking ahead for me. They seem to think they have something that everybody wants. What a dangerous thought to have. I suppose Mengele felt the same way." He now sat easily and tightly between the two boys on the lush sofa. *"I gave it thought, of course; after all, whatever sexual impulse we have is not something we ever invented for ourselves, is it? If it were, then we would be our own God, I suppose. Don't you find that we are all physically designed to experiment with sex? Yet at the same time so much ... prohibition ... is placed on doing whatever comes naturally. The prohibition only comes from people who'd love to do whatever it is you're doing, but they just haven't got the nerve. Why would the Church have any interest whatsoever in what I do in the privacy of my own home? I don't poke my nose into anyone else's affairs ... that often. You see, if you believe in a divine creator then you can ... **not** ... believe that he or she did **not** create what is monotonously known as sexual deviance ... How can I be deviating from something that I hadn't ever felt in the first place ... for there's no point in allotting a person with feelings that he would be con-demned to enact. Imagine having two perfectly healthy legs yet never using them – forever sliding about on your belly. I am God's design just as much as anyone else – I wasn't created by Walt Disney ... I'd be far more exciting if I had been. When I was a child my uncle asked me what I'd like to be when I grew up, and I didn't say to him 'Well, I'd like very much to be a sexual deviant, hounded for my thoughts alone, not having actually done anything yet hounded for having entertained the thought ... which is apparently just as bad as action.' I have found, you see, throughout my rather silly life, that there is very little difference between religion and racism. Both are the exact same torrent of intolerance. Now,"* he said, slyly glancing at his watch, *"I really am not one to waffle on, and since the object of this night is ... well, seduction ... do you mind if we now talk* *in plain language? You wouldn't be offended? I could quote* The Tempest *until the cows come home, of course, but unfortunately the cows do, at some point, come home ... if my bathroom mirror is anything to go by. Alas, Marjorie Main died in vain ... but at least Marie Dressler, er ... didn't. Now!"* He gulped the last drop of his vodka. Isaac was now ready for a playful beating, and it scarcely mattered what with.

"Why did you kill Noah Barbelo?" jumped in Nails.

"Ah! I thought your flanks of beef were somewhat too good to be true," said Isaac, not at all ruffled. He stood up and placed his empty glass on a side table. *"Before I explain, do you mind if I have another? Another liver, that is, and I might as well pour myself a tiny triple whilst I'm at it ..."*

"We don't mind," said Justy, and Isaac moved slowly to the drinks cabinet which spilled into the room from behind the lavish, deep couch of willowy propped cushions, and foolishly the boys took their eyes off Isaac for one sinister minute, which was all it took for Isaac to firmly grip two heavy Dom Perignon bottles at the neck and crash both with onerous impact onto the quartered heads of Nails and Justy, who barely moved on impact, who barely hummed a pained groan, and who took a second and heavier crash – each so deathly that both boys fell forwards in silent slow motion as if accepting holy communion. Preciously kneeling on the upper-crust carpeting, the boys were inexpressive and almost beloved, as Isaac managed a third and then a fourth deathblow that finished off both Nails and Justy with a cosy killer's cuddle. How on earth could it possibly have been so easy? Isaac summoned the strength from somewhere deeper than hell, and both Nails and Justy were far too trusting and paid the price. Removed

from life, Nails and Justy entered a blissful illumination underneath – yet not inside – the mind, archangels of the soul in a forward march of time, having lived now-complete lives without ever having said what was very truly on their minds. Reliable, yes, but not always very wise, and now the absolute death awareness sounded in their inner ears as all physical vibrations understood with some awe, and there was a voice with a certain sound like a lovers' understanding; finally desire both ways. Hypnotic rhythm tapped into Nails' brain – where, after all, everything is recorded. Justy felt a strong articulation of feeling; stomach, breast, mouth, ears, each sinking into a lone cry of despair. Cardsharp Isaac stood above both boys as they lay together, their bodies closing down. *"My strength, you see, is quite ridiculously underrated,"* Isaac mumbled, *"and who would ever guess that I scarcely know what I'm doing? But still, if you wish to attain your beloved God then ... why not die? Why not rush to meet him? Why hang about here ... where no one is ever willing to die ... even at that moment when they are ... unavoidably dying? Oh, just look at this mess ... and my best carpet, too."*

A cool wind blows us back across town, where Eliza and Ezra remain a valid portrait of vibrating goodness and crushing love, flopped as they were around each other, with stark lighting immunizing the basement scene; and all of their being passed between them as cluttered school emblems wrinkled and crinkled on the walls, and bicycles and sports racquets crowded in corners. Warm though the basement was, it was not without small touches of freshly cut flowers and elegant side-lamps. Perhaps it's just another folksy Saturday night of warm cooking smells and one-line jokes as all the senses are ministered to, snugger than bugs in rugs. Their emotions deepen whilst together, and the rest of their race are lesser lights – never flashing, always socially unspoken, without craft, unable to correct themselves. Eliza and Ezra curl up on the couch ready to give whatever can be given, all open between them. Ezra has changed, though, a crack of duress and the sight of Noah Barbelo and the crippled flatfoots being neither police nor force; Isaac's suspicious-looking friends shielding him as if vocation taught them nothing else, for they shared his tastes in all things. Realism in abundance sustained Ezra and Eliza in equal measure, since they now knew and feared too much – the facts of life and death now dominated by a new moral obligation that doubled their thinking process; and all around them there is media praise for people who just did not matter, yet always-ready criticism for those who would dare suggest that life could quite easily be far more civilized. *What is this terrible, terrible world? And how are we expected to behave within it? The doom of the universe all around us, yet the impossibility of touching the heart's desire.*

"The United States Constitution says that all men are born free and equal," started Eliza, *"but no mention of women."*

"I think it's implied, men means men and womb-men," said Ezra, without much confidence.

"But it doesn't say so," Eliza bats back.

"No, but mankind means everyone, not just men," replied Ezra.

"Then why not say so? Why not say 'humankind' instead of 'mankind'? For example, the Constitution doesn't say 'all women are created equal' whilst assuming that we'd all understand this to include men as well as women. The word 'woman' is never used to also include men, so why should we assume the word 'man' to include women? We shouldn't, and it didn't and it doesn't."

"Well," laughed Ezra, *"if I say 'c'mon, you guys,' I'm not necessarily addressing just guys. I could be talking to guys and girls, but everyone knows I mean everyone."*

"I understand. But would you address the same crowd and say 'c'mon, you girls'? No, you wouldn't, because men are insulted to be addressed as female, whilst women are thought to be delighted to be addressed as guys."

"Hang the innocent!" struck Ezra. They both kissed, but Eliza was impatient to return to the conversation.

"Do you think Elizabeth Barbelo is watching us now, and if she is, why doesn't she appear?"

"I ache in every muscle when I think of that night," said Ezra. *"The question wasn't ... answerable ... I'd been shoved past my limits ... I know that. Do you think I haven't cried every single night? Something corrupt happened to all of us, and it began that day in the woods with that schizo hobo. We didn't mean to kill him, but that would be a lame confession to any jury. It's between me and God Almighty now, I know that,"* and with this Ezra's tears lightly reappeared. *"I don't understand anything any more. I've never been a party to violence of any kind, and now I've killed a man and hidden his body in the woods ... and then I dig up the body of a young boy murdered twenty years ago, and I'm unable to manage the truth to anyone ... walking around in a hypnotic state ... hearing Harri's voice wherever I go. Edgar Allan Poe couldn't concoct this. And in the midst of it all I was meant to lead a relay team to national ... televised victory!"*

Cautiously, Eliza unwound herself from Ezra and stood up. A trance switched her expression to shock.

"What – are – you – talking – about?" She towered above coiled Ezra. *"You have ... murdered someone?"*

"Yes. He attacked me, and then my punch was too forceful and

he ... just ... died ... hidden in ferns and fauna and woodland shit ... never discovered."

"Which is ... a good thing?" Eliza asked in disbelief.

"Eliza, don't. I can hear it in your voice. Don't scrutinize ... you know me as someone who is personally good, and I did what I had to do, please believe me, and I've cried myself to a state of exhaustion every night since. Nails, Harri, Justy – they weren't to blame, but they stood by me, and I'll never again know mental rest. Yet I have no understanding of why what happened took place. There's no answer. Yet it had to be done. There's a point at which you do what you must to protect yourself, and there isn't time to consider implications or tolerance or holy scriptures or nineteenth-century laws ... it's all there in the pit of the stomach, and you articulate whatever it is you're feeling, whether it be with words or actions, and to hell with the Pope – who, in any case, isn't there, isn't facing whatever it is you face, and we must make the best of what we feel. Eliza, you are looking at me with gunfire in your unendurably beautiful eyes, yet you and only you have saved me through these recent weeks. We all have only one chance at living. Please don't seal away our chance of happiness ... if there could be any changing of your mind now –"

"But you have done to this hobo precisely what Isaac did to Noah! You killed someone and hid the body! Are you insane? I've protected you, yes, but without knowing any of this!" Eliza was now shouting.

"Eliza, don't! If you stand in opposition to me then I'm finished. The two situations have no similarity whatsoever."

"But two people are dead, and their murderers are intent on getting along undiscovered ... Ezra, what gives you this utopian spirituality? What is so superior in your defense against this hobo? And what do you even know about Noah Barbelo ... that he wasn't a sly boy who coaxed Dean Isaac into some blackmail act *of opportunism? You read of these cases and the adult is always thought to be at fault ... but these kids ... they're not all purified little tender angels ... they know what sex is and how to use it and they know how adults are trapped and guilty and doomed as soon as the whistle is blown. Kids know all these consequences, and they know how to bow their heads and tremble in a courtroom ... the gaze fixed down, the confused blink of the eyes, the pursed mouth of confusion."*

"You're wrong! You're wrong! I saw this boy's mother! Her predicament had destroyed her, and mothers know their sons!"

Eliza collapsed into an armchair and wept. Sammy suddenly burst in. Ezra threw an atlas towards Sammy's head that directly hit the target, and Sammy withdrew, impaired.

"And I thought I was entangled in enough, but now you've told me this I become ... a conspirator, a schemer ... unless I blab to the flatfoots."

Ezra knelt before her. *"Your emotional permanence is all that keeps me level. I only learned to love because you showed me that I could. Nothing else in life is enough. I will give you no trouble for the rest of our lives. I beg you to take me as I am, with the knowledge of all that's happened. The agony will only be sharper if we separate. Unless I am with you I shall never be where I belong. Together we can recover, and we can live a happy life. There is no one but you for whom I feel this love. I'd endure any pain in order to spare you from it. Your love is beyond price. I am so heartily sorry for all that has taken place, but I am spared further self-hatred if I can turn around and there you are."*

"Yes, there I am ... co-conspirator," she is now calming her anger.

"Don't make this our parting moment. I can't bear anything more than I already have. Life has been ... disgusting ... no point and

no purpose. I am puzzled, I am repulsed, my brain doesn't stop this inane chatter … I am guilty, I am innocent, I'm relied upon … and all I await is for your arm to come around my shoulder, and love streams out of me. I've done nothing wrong."

His speech now over, Ezra lowered his head and Eliza softly placed her right hand upon it, reassuringly, for she now has little hope of anything at all, but she has nothing to gain from leaving Ezra.

"I wasn't attacking," she said, *"I was trying to clarify."* Ezra looked up, elated to the point of tears, for he had heard understanding in her voice.

"I didn't murder that mutant … I was simply defending myself against what he was about to do to me."

"Perhaps. But you know the courts of justice, and only a fool could have faith in such bird turd. Justice and the law are two entirely different things."

If true love takes the bad days in the same spirit as the good days, then the love of Ezra and Eliza now faced its final test. At ease, they rocked gently together, resuming their love. With her wish to spend the night in her own bed, Ezra drove Eliza the few drowsy blocks towards her parents' home. Although they had nothing to say to one another, what was not said indicated a return to hearts possessed, for their past pride and joy had always indicated a love that could last longer than life – alas, one of the imperialist tricks of romance. The quiet streets were sleepwalking with secrets, the night resting with an inability to whisper, the traffic lights changing without any sign of traffic – their reds and greens talking to no one, fresher air creeping in to disadvantage the impurities of the deadened day. All quiet, all still in this decent and pleasant atmosphere of slumber and repose, where lush houses of beddy-bye shut-eye snoozled in sleepland; a smiling sleep of dreamland. In the middle of a cross-street the hypnotic sedation exploded as an automobile self-propelled itself from nowhere and cannoned into the passenger side of Ezra's car with a sledgehammer smash that folded Eliza into the warped dashboard as she died instantly, head bowed into shattered glass. Ezra fell out of the wreckage and crunched against concrete, as the running feet of the slayer driver were heard darting away from the smashup; that tone, that sound and the silence that surrounded it, the shabby soles of shoes, evidence to be denied, Eliza no longer in possession of thought or those gifts and gestures bestowed at birth. Muscles, voice – all gone, Eliza denied of her revenge, drifting out of this world and no longer in anyone's way, as permanent twilight called to her like the next dance step. But the cheated victim was Ezra once again, condemned to life.

The true origin of the word 'hero' does not carry connotations of either honor or virtue. A legend is something that might be true or false, and a conundrum is an answer that provides a joke, but generations shift word-definitions in order to suit whatever suits. In a listless dream state, catatonic Ezra is bedded for the unforeseeable narcotized term at the University Hospital following excessive psychosomatic treatments. The transient trackster's pleasures roll speedily through his incapacitated mind, for he has fallen to the reality that very few can bear – of being enfeebled to a desensitized and spiritless resignation. Traumatism has left him frostbitten and chilblained, feverous and flushed, fiery and felled. Delirium has lowered his resistance, and wired-up to the constant blips and blips and tings of surgical machinery his soft face leans sideways … staring out of the window towards the full extent of freedom. As long as he can see out there he is not in here. Attending examiners burst into the room, and nursing sisters whip around Ezra's bed with their certain perspectives and their reams of stress tests and scribbled diagnostics, yet oddly saying nothing at all if asked for information. Ezra's playful days are over, and blood-counts replace them; time, once a gift, is now a punishment. What you have been saved for has had its curtain call. Everything begins in the mind but ends with the body. These, now, are the weakly peaky backroads – under the weather and out of sorts, as white as a measly sheet. No computer-assisted tomography, no heat therapy, no sweat therapy, no urinalysis … nothing, now, can save the airsick slide of the suicidalist. He was once important only because the life within him had importance … but when lack of safety is suddenly nothing to fear? When the will finally gives out, and wants no return? No further tears against the dying of the light, as the quiet exit becomes the logical perspective. The practical nurse of title (but no apparent function) pounds noisily about the room, checking numbers and speaking loudly, not allowing Ezra any sleep, yet his nothingness has already taken him far away from medical examinations and sodium drips and the morbid aspect of badly paid caregivers with their podgy blue hands and their tense understanding – momentarily funny, yet without a breath of tolerance. How to rescue the soul? We suffer only because we believe we are alone, but how to get through without faith in life?

Why should Ezra wait any longer – seeing Eliza's smashed face before him and Harri's grave beside him … and the missing Nails and the lost Justy, neither ever seen again on a landscape of far too many strange shadows. As Isaac settled down with a frothy Mimosa, the Lausanne sun warmed up considerably and he at the very least felt grateful for the black-hand syndicate that secured his protection. Here in Lausanne he would begin his memoirs, as most do when all's been done. There were solitary figures idling by the Ouchy bay, and surely the law of averages would prompt at least one of them towards an assenting nod, if only as a basic half-amused act of human kindness.

Ezra's eyes lowered at the coming of nightfall, with all of its secrets of anonymity. A light from the yard at the back of the hospital threw darting shadows, yet anything recognized by Ezra tortured him, for his body had now absented whilst wondering why it hadn't been allowed to die, and *who is it that keeps forcing me back?* Figuratively he had indeed already died – our great stylist of the track leaned into a rolling and groaning Harri trembling with exhaustion after a lengthy run and now lying flat on his back on the sun-soaked track, and Ezra kissed him softly on the head and Harri looked up with eyes that shed a gentle melancholy at an affection so unexpected and one that moves different people in different ways. The body at unguarded moments is fully alive to accept more readily, and will not be guided by jealous advice.

"May we never be apart," Ezra sensitively murmured to Harri, knowing that love could never be experienced without risk, or without a voice with a certain sound. There

were days when … all we needed to do was accept, irresponsible acts meaning not very much at all, a disassembled life with a head full of music and a heart full of hope.

"People reveal themselves only when they make love," mused Eliza, chewing on a pencil in Ezra's memory, *"and never at any other time. Which is not something you can raise a toast to, unfortunately. I wonder why we're all so lifeless? This humdrum civility … what is it? All of us crying to be let out! Well, I have a theory, of course …"*

"Somehow I thought you might," came Ezra with a pretend sigh, but so happy to spread out on the lawn at his parents' house, the half-asleep sound of mating doves in evening discourse without a single false note.

"Well," began Eliza, *"once you finally know someone intimately … they no longer have any defense against you … and you suddenly have power over them … the power to hurt them quite viciously …"*

"But why would you want to?"

"Well, that's the heavy burden of heavy petting, isn't it?" she said, gibbering now into Ezra's dreams, where he no longer needed to keep his sanity unclouded as he felt the pull of the earth. A shivery touch brought him back … back to where everyone lived permanently on the point of apology, and a physician's voice chattered and chirped with sharpened senses of noisy self-deception. Oh, the limited human mind, smiled Ezra. How it cannot keep pace! How we scamper about, trying to manage our lives properly … we little ripples … who go, and try our measly best to drag everything with us.

"You can tell everything about a person just by looking at their hands," offered Nails, one distant genial Saturday at Ledger's Bar, yet no convincing account followed. I was there,

thought Ezra, and I loved, and I welcomed with gratitude, and I cracked the female mystery wide open, and the love of my friends lived rent-free in my heart, and I ran on that track like a whole person – never asking for more than there was … ice-cold mornings made me laugh, so happy was I then. True friendship is a miracle; 'yes' is always a smile, but events outstrip us all sooner or later, and what happens when you are unable to call out? Who, even, to call to? Tonight, Ezra had exhausted himself knowing that his frail walk to this very bed had been his final walk to anywhere. Oh, let me sleep now, without any chance stirrings, without the pointless yap of EMTs, this heart exhausted and resolved, and it wants its turn of a replacement for life, no longer awaiting answers, too psychologically wounded to bother with questions, no longer disputing the Death Card already dealt. The lazily scrubbed hygiene of this little white room! Yet what of the spiritual hygiene approaching? The stove has died quietly, the palms of the dying are open flatly, and this murderous planet of criminal nations is a joy to leave behind. It is always Saturday in my mind's eye, he thinks, as his breathing now comes from somewhere deeper than his chest, all lust and trust behind him, but happy to be giving in to something stronger than himself – just for this one time. How many doctors does it take? Why do I now remember things that I never actually knew? Come on, that's enough for now. Close your book in this faltering light, for your eyes are pinkish and tired, little man. There is school tomorrow, and the day after, and the day after, and the day after. Destiny, now, has nothing to do with you, Ezra – all responsibility shredded and shed. Yet there at the foot of his bed he could clearly see a full materialization of the phantomic wretch; the stumbling unearthly midget whose life had been ended by one concentrated punch of self-defence from Ezra … that richly mind-swilling day in the woods as we all lived our small lives. Yet here he was again – at the foot of the bed, like a barking dog … like a smiling and shadowy disembodied seething mess, watching Ezra slide away, the wretch with a look of order and meaning upon his boiling face of inscrutable threat, with all the superior rectitude and militancy of a priest administering the last rites. Ezra applied final will to fully recognize the spectral sheet, as maddening midnight church bells provided their harmonized soothing dullness, asking only that we remember with kindness.